D1462661

GRETE WEIL was born in 1906. She studied German literature in Berlin, Munich, and Frankfurt. In 1932, she married Edgar Weil, a theatrical producer at the Munich Kammerspiele. In 1935, the couple emigrated to Holland. After the German invasion of the Netherlands, however, they were unable to flee, and in 1941 Edgar Weil was taken to the concentration camp in Mauthausen, where he was killed.

Grete Weil worked with the Jewish Council in Holland, but went underground in the fall of 1943...and survived. In 1947, she returned to Germany, where she was married to the opera director Walter Jokisch.

While Grete Weil lived in hiding in Holland, she began a novel, STREETCAR-STOP BEETHOVENSTRAAT (1963); a libretto for Hans Werner Henze's opera, BOULEVARD SOLITUDE (1951); and a collection of short stories, HAPPY—SAID UNCLE (1968). In addition, Weil is a busy translator and critic. She now lives near Munich.

Avon Books are available at special quantity discounts for bulk purchases for sales promotions, premiums, fund raising or educational use. Special books, or book excerpts, can also be created to fit specific needs.

For details write or telephone the office of the Director of Special Markets, Avon Books, Dept. FP, 1790 Broadway, New York, New York 10019, 212-399-1357.

MY SISTER, MY ANTIGONE

GRETE WEIL

Translated from the German by
KRISHNA WINSTON

A BARD BOOK/PUBLISHED BY AVON BOOKS

MY SISTER, MY ANTIGONE is an original publication of Avon Books. This work has never before appeared in book form.

AVON BOOKS
A division of
The Hearst Corporation
1790 Broadway
New York, New York 10019

Copyright © 1984 by Grete Weil
Translation Copyright © 1984 by Avon Books
Published in arrangement with the author
Library of Congress Catalog Card Number: 83-90406
ISBN: 0-380-85522-4

All rights reserved, which includes the right to reproduce this book or portions thereof in any form whatsoever except as provided by the U.S. Copyright Law. For information address Benziger Verlag, Zurich, c/o Joan Daves, 59 East 54th Street, New York, New York 10022

First Bard Printing, January, 1984

BARD TRADEMARK REG. U.S. PAT. OFF. AND IN OTHER COUNTRIES, MARCA REGISTRADA, HECHO EN U.S.A.

Printed in the U.S.A.

OP 10 9 8 7 6 5 4 3 2 1

MY SISTER,

MY ANTIGONE

1

As I wake up, a sentence flashes through my mind, making me almost giddy with happiness: *Today everything is about to begin.* Even though I do not know what *everything* means, or *begin*, the thought produces a sense of well-being. I revel in it until I am completely awake and conscious. Then it dawns on me that nothing is about to begin; on the contrary, everything—and now this *everything* comes into clear focus as everything connected with my own life—is grinding to a halt. I am old, an old woman. Not *very* old, just *quite* old. Quite: my escape hatch. A very narrow opening. Does *relatively* have a better sound to it? Or: *You are only as old as you feel?* One moment that can mean one hundred, the next twenty. In the moment of waking it was twenty; and, after the shock of recognition, around seventy. As old as my years. Simply *old*.

My morning devotions: I rattle off the names of my dead. My dog's name last. Now even my dog is gone. A few months back he failed to return from his evening run. Killed or stolen. Dead for me, at any rate. I am alone, having moved back to Frankfurt as I do every fall, exchanging the house in the Swiss Ticino region where I rattle around for the apartment where I also rattle around.

I reach for my hearing aids, lying on the nightstand. As I fit them into my ears, one of them emits a shrill peep. Once I have adjusted the volume, I can hear the traffic in the streets below. To me this noise, which others abhor, is welcome. These little devices, complicated electronic receivers in flesh-colored plastic shells, have drawn me back into the world.

I get up, run a bath, and lie motionless in the bubbles and warm water, once more young. In a few weeks I mean to go skiing. The lift attendant will shove me on my way with a respectful "Keep up the good work, ma'am." He wants to pay me a compliment and instead hurts me to the quick. They all hurt me. My contemporaries with their endless whining about their ailments, their loneliness. The forty- and fifty-year-olds who erect a barrier between themselves and me, a barrier in whose shelter they can do all the things I am supposed to be incapable of now. The young ones—"a terrible generation," according to Trudy, whom I call a friend only because we shared a desk in elementary school. "What do you see in them?—usually you're so choosy. They don't wash, they won't work."

"I just happen to like them. They have such lovely long hair."

"You can't be serious! You mean you find all that scraggly hair beautiful?"

"I do, and what's more, I'd love to plunge my hands into it."

"Into the boys' hair?"

"The girls' too. But I'd prefer the boys'."

Queer old duck, Trudy must think. And the young folk? Much gratitude I can expect from them. They reject people like me out of hand. Their eyes are wary. And why should they trust us? Us of all people? The Nazi generation. The generation of SS officers, execution squad commanders, concentration camp guards.

But I am Jewish. One of the victims. Most of them fall silent when they hear that. Some of them ask questions, want to know what it was like before '33. How soon we realized what was up. What made us decide to emigrate. Whether we were allowed to take anything with us. How our neighbors behaved. Our friends. Whether we knew about the suppression of the Left. Whether we never considered resisting.

No, the thought never crossed our minds. We had not been brought up to defend ourselves. Our parents were convinced they had smoothed the path for us. In this modern, progressive world their children's Jewishness would never be used against them. We were rooted in that belief.

The curse of roots. Daughter of a *Geheimrat,* a princess who never has to lift a finger. Her bed is made for her, the table set, clothes laundered, rips mended. Taken to and from school by a nanny. Later, when there is no longer a nanny, a weary maid is there waiting outside the theater, the concert hall. The dog is fed by the cook, the cat's litter box emptied by the housemaid. Mother selects suitable clothes, Father supervises the homework. Everything runs like clockwork. A so-called good education, incorporating all the clichés, the standard thought patterns of the nineteenth century.

The bubbles have dissolved. I convert the bath sponge into a toy boat, pushing it forward, around in a circle, back to me. I have done this for as long as I can remember, the only interruption being the time I spent in hiding and the long period after that when I had no bathtub. Such a familiar game, yet suddenly I am swept by that sense of strangeness that overtakes me so often these days. A strangeness that eludes clear definition but seems to be growing steadily. A

9

sense of distance between myself and others, myself and objects.

I climb out of the tub, slip into my bathrobe, and put on the kettle in the kitchen to boil water for coffee. I smear a slice of bread with cottage cheese and jam, and swallow a handful of many-colored pills—to improve my blood circulation, prevent vitamin and calcium deficiencies, strengthen my heart, and generally counteract wear and tear. I have no idea whether they do any good. If I did not take them, perhaps my hearing would be even worse, perhaps I would have had a heart attack long since, could no longer go skiing. But do I really still have the stamina for skiing? And then, of course, there is my horror of the crowded slopes, of the daredevils, my fear of breaking something. Does this mean one more pleasure I shall have to forego?

I take my medication without placing much faith in it, like the atheist who sends for a priest when he is dying because one can never be sure. More and more now I catch myself doing things I scoff at if I see others doing them.

After breakfast back to the bathroom. I comb my hair. Thick gray hair, nothing to be ashamed of. Wrinkles everywhere, on my forehead, around my eyes. Deep furrows extending from either side of my nose to the corners of my mouth. When I smile I look younger. So I smile. Smile into the mirror, although I know it creates a false impression by insisting on showing a frontal view of my face. Should I purchase a triple mirror? Even more depressing. I admonish myself to cultivate illusion, not to destroy it. To smooth on lotion and moisturizer, apply color. All these rituals I have performed so often, preparing for caresses, for kisses. Now I still go through the motions. With no one there to admire the results, and no one in sight. No one for whom I make myself beautiful.

Once dressed I sit down at my desk. Type out a few letters, attending only to what is most urgent. I postpone the personal letters. People write to ask how I am, how I can stand it all alone in the city. I have little desire to tell others about myself. Should I write: Dear X (it is mostly women who express concern about me), You ask what I am up to. Nothing worth mentioning. I am alive and kicking. I go for walks, almost always downtown; I find the parks boring without a dog. You wonder, no doubt, why I subject myself to all that ugliness. Well, you see, I have a special fondness for ugly streets. And I am taking the easy way out—there are so many of them. I might go so far as to say almost all of them are ugly. I hate those streets that are famous for their beauty, like the Champs-Elysées. Beautiful streets would make it impossible for me to concentrate on my lessons, which deal with heart attacks, brain tumors, cancer of the stomach, emphysema. It is important that I learn these lessons by heart; I need them constantly for discussing my friends' ailments with them.

The elevator carries me down seven floors to the lobby, where I fish my newspaper out of the mailbox. Reading the paper has not become quite such an addiction as watching television, but it still offers a certain satisfaction, even though the news is anything but satisfactory. I like to know what is going on, always did. Even as a child I would fly into a rage if something were kept from me. I spend about an hour on the paper, even reading the classified section in my reluctance to be done. Finally I fold up the paper and put it down on the end table by the sofa.

I go into the kitchen again. Since nothing else appeals to me at the moment, I spread another slice of

11

bread with cottage cheese and jam. Jam is caloric, cottage cheese is not. As if the two canceled each other out, I eat with gusto, then grumpily go back to my desk.

If I still had my dog it would be time for his walk now. But he is gone, and I do not feel in the mood to go out alone. I try to think of someone I could call up, dial Trudy's number, let the phone ring a long time, realize she is not at home, and hang up.

Now it has happened in spite of me: I have thought about my dog and cannot stop thinking about him. Tears well up, and I whisper to myself, "Old Mother Hubbard went to the cupboard to get her poor dog a bone . . ." He tilts his brown head to one side and gazes up at me with his amber eyes, as if to ask what in the world I am trying to tell him. The last being who was all mine, who needed me, whom I fed and doted on, who gave me a reason for living, whom I failed, all because I could not bring myself to say no, out of an indolence I pretended was love.

"Don't you ever chain him?" the stout innkeeper asked. "He's always loitering around my Bella."

"Oh, sometimes I do," I lied; actually I would not have dreamed of interfering with his freedom and his interest in Bella. A dog lives dangerously, that's all. Better a short, intense life than a long, dreary one. So easy to say. But then, when he failed to return . . . No, I am sure he did not let anyone steal him. Nor did he run away, or certainly no farther than to Bella, who lived at most five minutes from my house. If only I had found his body. If only I were sure he had been run over. Unbearable to think that someone might have shot him. Or clubbed him to death. Or given him a piece of poisoned meat. My murder complex. My old wound.

With trepidation I reach for the black notebook

with the working title *Antigone* on the cover, open it, and read over the last few pages I wrote. None of it any good. I tear out the pages and put them next to the notebook, planning to rework them. But I am not in the mood.

Tired again already, I yawn, lie down on the sofa, pull the afghan up to my chin and let my thoughts dwell on my princess, my favorite plaything for longer than I can remember. I do not recall when and where we first met. Was it my father, with his classical education and his belief that the world was intact and meaningful, who introduced me to her, or my big brother, who after four years in the trenches in France no longer harbored any illusions? He told hilarious and thrilling stories about the Nibelungs, Lohengrin, Don Carlos, Sherlock Holmes, Old Shatterhand, and the Countess Geschwitz. But how about Antigone? No, he would have found her too serious, a bore; that kind of single-mindedness left him cold. Did I hear about her from my red-bearded German teacher, Emeran Kajetanus, on whom I had a crush, or from his unspeakably stupid predecessor, whose history lessons followed the German nationalist creed to the letter? Perhaps I was not even introduced to her, but saw her name on a theater program or the spine of a book? Did I read about her in Schwab's *Most Beautiful Legends of Classical Antiquity?* Or did I come upon her later, in the works of the poet Friedrich Hölderlin? I do not know. What I do know is that for a long while I simply accepted her fate, as if it were self-explanatory, a grim story, no more. I felt no particular affinity for her. Even when I was at the university, cavalierly tossing around terms like ''Oedipus complex'' and ''repression,'' I viewed her as just one of four children born of a union that impressed me tremendously because it was so scandalous. Not until I was

13

brutally jerked out of my own princesslike existence, brought face to face with murder and annihilation, did the figure of Antigone undergo a change for me, becoming larger, more significant, more luminous, more ambiguous. Now I recognized her self-destructiveness, her incestuous passion for Polyneices, a kind of vanity, and the arrogance characteristic of martyrs, who rightly or wrongly consider themselves superior to others. I tried to write her story, but all I produced was a pretentious sentimental epic on a heroic maiden. Yet I did not give up; there was always an Antigone notebook on my desk, alongside my other projects.

How do I see her? One day I think I have her, the next day the certainty eludes me. At times she is part of me, at other times my exact opposite. A dream over time, the image of what I wish to be but am not, a king's daughter in her early years, then a vagabond, an unyielding resistance fighter who stakes her life and loses, a disciple and beloved of Dionysus, for whom life means hate and death means love, a determined soul who refuses to deviate from her own law.

I sketch out a conversation here, jot down an episode there—I have never got beyond the preliminaries. If I lie on the sofa as I am doing now, if I go out for a walk, she is there, and everything is clear between us; I know where we stand, no doubts assail me. She has on the yellow dress she knows I like. She is good company, like all people who love life. Yes, she loves life, in spite of her yearning for death. If she did not, I would not find her longing for death credible, would see it as the superficial chatter of a malcontent. She speaks of her wanderings through the mountains, the fishermen among whom she and Oedipus lived during part of their exile. She tells of Athens, the elegant metropolis, of its clever king, Theseus. Although there is an air of sorrow that never quite leaves her, she is quick-witted and funny. Moreover, you cannot put anything over on her. Her deed is a brilliant piece of theatrics. Planned down to the smallest detail. Executed with prodigious determination. She sneaks out under the cover of darkness to where Polyneices lies unburied. The guards' torches flicker, shadows flutter over the ground, wisps of mist float upward. She cautiously hops from one stone to the next so as to leave no footprints. She is light-footed, moves quietly; yet on a perfectly still night she could be heard. But luck is with her, the bit of luck one needs to carry off a grand scheme. The men are singing to keep themselves awake. A few paces from the body the stones run out. She goes up on tiptoe. Five or six steps to the corpse, steps that leave no recognizable tracks; no human being, no animal makes such tracks—let them think it is magic. A signal—hark!—the supernatural has occurred—a miracle—fall to your knees—cover your faces—weep, weep for this dead man, weep for your city. Protest, protest! Dust over her dead brother, quickly, lest she be interrupted. No burial this, but then why should it be, that is not what matters. Unseen, she slips back into the city.

Day arrives, the long, bright day, and in the brilliant sunlight she goes forth again, a circlet of poppies in her dark hair, adorned for the sacrifice she intends to make for the city, for the people, in the name of justice. She sees the corpse, dragged free of its thin covering of dust, sees it, does not see it, cannot make herself look at the wound, the shattered chest. She pulls up clods of earth with her bare hands, throws dirt on the bloody flesh, uttering shrill cries like a terrified bird. Everything goes as she hoped: she is seized, dragged before Creon, who interrogates her before all the people—and that is the main thing; now at last she has a chance to say her piece: *Not for hatred but for love am I among you.* Sometimes I also think of the line as it is usually quoted: *I cannot share in hatred, but in love.* But I prefer Hölderlin's lonelier, more arrogant version. Anyone who associates anything at all with her name always quotes that line. Her principle, the source of her fame. In that line she formulated a moral standard without invoking God, a thing very rarely achieved.

I simply do not believe her contention that in her raging pain she really cared what happened to his corpse. "The most terrible thing," says my Dutch cleaning lady, Mevrouw Bartjes, when Waiki has been murdered at the Mauthausen concentration camp, "is that he has no grave." No, that is the only thing that is not terrible. An abyss between Mevrouw Bartjes and me, the differences in our backgrounds and upbringing, our very being, the way we perceive things. Mevrouw Bartjes weeps and I weep, Mevrouw Bartjes suffers and I suffer, Mevrouw Bartjes no longer understands the world, and I have never understood it.

No grave, and if he had one, I would not visit it. I do not want to stand there, with the frightful guilty conscience of the survivor, looking at a tidy little garden plot. I do not need this meaningless bit of ground, which we never set foot on together, which has nothing to do with our love. Even without any reminder I keep asking myself: Why did I fail to keep you back when you wanted to go out into the streets in the middle of a raid? Why did we believe the woman who warned you when she said they only took those young men who were inside buildings? Why did I not hide you in a chest, or persuade you to climb onto the flat roof on which our dormer looked out; it ran across the entire block, past many windows

16

behind which lived Dutch people willing to help. Why did I listen to my anxiety dream in which two policemen hurled you down from this roof, why?

No grave, no funeral celebration. Why do people celebrate death? The soothing, comforting words of the minister, who did not know the departed; the soothing, hypocritical words of superiors and fellow workers. A last triumph of disregard for the individual, inane pieties, completely interchangeable. Black dresses—they are becoming to most women—black ties and mourning bands. The pallbearers knock over one of the candelabra, the band makes a hash of the funeral march, a child refuses to let go of the shovel meant for throwing earth into the grave, a person unconnected with the whole business expresses his condolences to another person unconnected with the whole business. Hands are shaken, eyes are dabbed, noses are blown, appointments are made, business is transacted. Soon a marker will be placed on the grave, a name inscribed in gold: rest in peace for all eternity, for that eternity that lasts thirty years, perhaps even fifty, so long as someone continues to pay for the final resting place.

Urs has a grave. He died in the hospital while I was out in the corridor smoking a cigarette. Not because I did not know what was happening; I knew only too well, and I wanted to keep that crew with their oxygen masks, tubes, and injections away from his body, condemned to a death that brooked no resistance. When I came back into the room, he was dead. I saw it plainly, but tried nevertheless to feel his pulse. My own heart was pounding so hard that I could not have felt anything even if there had been anything to feel. Then I held the mirror of my compact to his lips; the glass remained unclouded. I turned away; I do not like to look at the dead—they are gone, once and for all. I could not cry either. So I stood there, staring into the dark window, feeling not desperate, not sad, merely empty. Gradually my mind began to function again, and I went to get the nurse's aide. He came on the run, felt the pulse, put his ear to Urs's heart, shook his head, said "He's dead," put his bony arms around me with a practiced gesture, led me to the only chair in the room, hurried out again, and returned with a crucifix and a lighted candle. When I said no, he took the crucifix away but left the candle. I walked around the bed and blew it out. "What shall I dress him in?" the aide asked, unsure of himself now.

"Leave him as he is." An uneasy look. Has she taken leave of her senses?

"But is it all right to wash him?"

"If you wish," I said, because I had no desire to argue with him. "I doubt that anyone washed Waiki."

"Pardon?"

"It doesn't matter to me whether you wash him." The room began to spin, and I sat down again.

Urs has a grave because in Germany you have to have a grave. Mevrouw Bartjes would have to admit that in this case it was the dying—even if it was a first-class death with all the comforts—that was really the most terrible part; there we would agree. But she would disapprove if she knew that I do not visit the grave, that I weep no tears over it, place no flowers on it, pluck off no withered leaves.

Thumbing one's nose at convention. Freedom. What is freedom, anyway? No fit state for the living. Life: an unremitting effort to destroy freedom. My freedom after Waiki's death destroyed by Urs, my freedom after Urs's death destroyed by the dog, and already I am thinking: If I were absolutely sure he was dead . . . No, no new dog. Even without one there are enough forces working to curtail my freedom. I must write to Ursula, to Milia, to Lorely, to Andreas, must call Gisela this evening after ten. Perhaps go out for a drink with Peter. Try again to reach Trudy. I implore each of them: Take a bit of my freedom. Just a little, I don't want to burden you, but still. You wouldn't want to spoil things for me, I know that. And I would so like to live. Just a bit longer. Let's get together soon. I'll hop in the car and visit you. Then in the summer you can come and stay with me. For two or three weeks. Of course I have the time. For you I always have time. Oh, my work—that's not so important. Besides, I can do my writing just as well with you there. And all the while I know I cannot. That I go shopping and cook and drive my friends around, because it is their vacation, after all, and I want them to have a good time. If only I had the courage to remain alone. But I do not.

Thumbing one's nose at convention. Deadly freedom. Antigone.

attack on chorus (humanity)

O tomb, O bridal chamber, and you, O house of stone, destined eternally to embrace me. Keep silent, press my lips together, bite them till they bleed, anything to avoid crying out. Refuse to give all of you the satisfaction. One need only look at you. Your dull faces. Your indifferent faces, which reveal that to you a death sentence means nothing more than an hour's diversion. Your lewd faces, your intent staring to see how the condemned person holds up. Your smug faces that say tomorrow is another day, and the day after, and all the next week. For you. You are not being walled up in a dark cave. You will not suffer hunger and thirst. Not you. Your self-righteous faces, your outrage at the attempt to bury Polyneices. You hypocrites. As if you cared about what happens to his corpse. Peace has come at long last, you can go about your business, lead your lethargic lives, what more do you ask? Polyneices' burial makes you neither richer nor poorer. Yet you shake your fists and mutter: Creon did the right thing. Utterly hopeless to try to make you see the inhumanity of his order, the baseness of his threat to kill anyone who disobeys him. In fact he was the only one who understood the significance of my protest. Still, he feels he must put on a show of power, display masculine firmness, protect the state and the gods. All this he needs in order to be able to face himself. But how about you? You find his actions perfectly in order; this is the order of things with which you feel comfortable, you yes-men, you time-servers, you parasites. Have you ever considered how awful it is to be killed? Certainly not when someone else's life was at stake. Have you ever wept a single tear of compassion? Are you even human? O people of Thebes! You know nothing, comprehend nothing. Neither the horror of dying, nor the great fulfillment of being with him for all eternity, of the same stuff as he.

Source?

She looked like him, was like him. Intelligent, headstrong, arrogant. Both of them grasped things quickly, reached decisions quickly, and acted quickly, impetuously. They stuck by one another and were prepared to defend each other against any attack. Their tragedy was not that they were brother and sister—there were ways around that taboo; after all, in Egypt the pharaohs married their sisters. It was not customary in Greece, but these two, who in any case never did the conventional thing, might have been the first. An insane undertaking: that a brother and sister, whose parents were mother and son, should beget children in turn, with the same traits, infinitely

20

heightened, refined. Pushing matters to their ultimate conclusion. Polyneices' breaking away and marrying the daughter of the King of Argos had less to do with love than with his ambition; he needed his father-in-law's army to wage war against Thebes. Probably he would have punished disobedience toward his orders as harshly as Creon, with whom he had much in common; perhaps Antigone would soon have found herself in conflict with King Polyneices. For that was their actual tragedy: that he thought in terms of the state, she in terms of freedom.

Why the devil do I want to write a book? Because I have to write, cannot live without writing? I can live without Waiki, something I would have thought impossible when he was still there, and without Urs, without my dog, without a child (which I never had), without my parents, without my childhood home, and without the Bavarian landscape. In order to earn money? If that were the case, I would have starved to death long ago. Do I wish to see my name in print, read reviews of myself in the paper, hear my own words being read by a stranger, or read them myself before a politely attentive audience? Do I want to invent answers for an interviewer who asks, ''Do you usually write in the morning or in the evening? Do you have the entire book sketched out in your mind before you begin? Do you belong to a literary group? Do you ever write poetry? What are your views on terrorism? Do you consider hashish more dangerous than alcohol and nicotine?''

No, I want none of that, at least not any longer; at one time I would have enjoyed it—perhaps—but in those days it never occurred to anyone to ask me about such things. When I was at the age at which one is flattered by such forms of recognition, the Third Reich descended upon us. We were searching for a way out of our prison, and I took up photography so as to be able to earn a living abroad. I worked as a photographer in Amsterdam until the Germans took away my studio. Then I went into hiding in an old house on a canal and could not be seen on the street because I would have been arrested and shipped off to Auschwitz.

"Why do you write?" a young American, a painter, asks me in Boston five minutes after we are introduced. I try to formulate an intelligent reply, but all that comes out are a few empty phrases about talent, the pleasure of imposing form on the recalcitrant material of experience, the desire to share one's insights—the things one says in such situations. I can tell she is not satisfied, so I explain that it is difficult for me to answer her question with sufficient precision in a foreign language. Excuses, lies—sometimes it is much easier to answer a question with precision in a foreign language. Under certain circumstances one can even say things one would never bring oneself to utter in one's own tongue—"I love you" in English, for example. Why do I write? Because, because . . . But even in English I do not know, cannot express what is so important about it to me. Would my desire to write be so urgent if my hearing were sharper? I do not know. Am I afraid of sinking into silence once and for all? I do not know.

I should like to write a book about a girl, a book which does not want to let me write it. I should like to compare her stubbornness with my own and see who finally gains the upper hand. Eventually she will have to answer me, explain why she staged this childish burial ceremony that helped no one, cost her her life, and left everything as before in Thebes. Why, if she was prepared to make any sacrifice, did she not kill

CRUCIAL QUESTION - will have to think about that for an eon or two.

Creon? Was she afraid of having to assume power herself? Was she afraid power would corrupt her?

To write a book about fear. Fear of death and fear of life; fear of dying tomorrow and fear of staying alive all day; fear of the cleaning lady who slams the door and fear that no one may be around to slam doors; fear of having to take a trip, of packing suitcases, calling a taxi, and fear of going nowhere, of always staying at home; fear of the television, with its torture, murders, executions in one's own living room, and the fear of no longer being able to distinguish between reality and fiction, between people condemned to death and actors portraying people condemned to death; fear that there may be no television, that the power may fail, that the set may break down; fear of illness, the hospital, the nurse who enters the room unheard and is suddenly standing there, the pain, the nausea, the bandages, the injections, the transfusions, the head physician who blares optimism in the direction of the bed and whispers laconic comments to the resident at his side, and fear of staying healthy, of always cooking one's own food, of doing all one's own errands and chores; fear of the children in the neighborhood who shout too loudly or speak too softly, and the fear that no children may be around, only a world of adults, ruled by the fear of not being the most successful, the healthiest, always first; fear of having to decide whether to purchase a new dog, to leave one city for another, to give up the house in the Ticino, and fear that everything may already be decided, that life will trickle away without any new challenges.

The bell rings twice, then a key turns in the lock. I jump up, fold the afghan, plump up the pillows, and run my hand over my hair. It is Christine, my godchild, a student of sociology, who rings the bell out of courtesy to announce her arrival, even though she has her own key, just in case I do not hear her ring. I want her to think I have been working—a holdover from childhood; whenever someone entered the room, I would quickly hide the book I had been reading and pull out my school notebook. By the time Christine knocks at the living room door, I am sitting at my desk, pen in one hand, cigarette in the other, and call to her to come in. She steps into the room, young and pretty in spite of a certain deliberate sloppiness. I lay down my pen, and she smiles—is it simple friendliness, or has she seen through me?—and then she asks, not too loudly and not too softly, with such clear diction that I can understand her effortlessly, "Am I interrupting your work, Auntie? So sorry." Then she comes closer, kisses me on the cheek, looks over my shoulder into the notebook, and says with a trace of impertinence, "Well, Auntie, how fares your noblest of virgins?"

2

Now this, on top of everything else: Christine, teasing me with an allusion to Hölderlin.

"You don't like her?" I ask irritably.

But she replies gently, "On the contrary, I like her very much. It's just that I feel terribly sorry for her, because she dies still a virgin."

"I'm not entirely certain that she does. Sometimes I let her taste tenderness in a man's arms."

"In spite of Sophocles and Hölderlin?"

"When I tell her story, she is my Antigone."

"Whom did she sleep with? With Polyneices?"

"No. That's what little sisters want, of course, but big brothers don't much like the idea."

"With Haemon?"

"He's such a namby-pamby."

Christine pulls up a chair, her blond hair falling over her face. Then she asks very delicately, "With Oedipus?"

"Come now, Christine. That sort of thing doesn't occur more than once in decent families." As I speak the words, I am thinking how beautiful it would be for Oedipus and Antigone to become lovers.

"I really want to know, Auntie. Who is it?"

"A shepherd."

"Ah, I see, the red princess. Tell me all about it." She gazes at me expectantly, like a child asking for a fairy tale. Will she have a tantrum if I refuse? I would, if I were she. But Antigone still belongs exclusively to me. It would be sheer folly to reveal my secret.

Keeping secrets: a habit formed early in life. Surrounding yourself with them, building a rampart of them, behind which you can live your own life. Practicing concealment, wearing masks, playing roles. No one has any right to know what you are really like.

If I had ever learned to open myself to others, I would let Christine see how happy her visit makes me. How much I need her. She is my link to a generation over which most of my contemporaries merely shake their heads. From her I learn many things I knew nothing of, things I need to know if I am to avoid total despair.

Today she is falling in with my game of hide-and-seek. Apparently she enjoys it, for she is becoming increasingly self-assured, while I grow less and less sure of myself. An unbroken series of false notes. Whites against blacks, emigrants against Germans, Germans against Jews from abroad—misunderstanding heaped upon misunderstanding. Every word I speak to Christine seems to imply: I have so much experience, and you have none. An assumption that forms a wall between us, preventing closeness from developing. I hear myself coming out with such apodictic statements as "That's what little sisters want." As if all little sisters wanted to sleep with their big brothers! Or: "That sort of thing doesn't occur more than once in decent families." Ha! Decent families! The language of the cultivated bourgeoisie in the pre-Hitler era. The refined turns of phrase used by a class-conscious group—in indecent families that sort of thing goes on all the time, or: You've heard about the Königs' carryings-on, haven't you, my dear? Confirmation that one belongs to the right circles.

"Auntie, tell me about the princess and the shepherd."

"Don't pester me," I say, trying to put her off and again striking a false note. "I'll show it to you when I have it written."

"But will you really write it? You say you *sometimes* let her taste tenderness. That means you don't always put that part in."

"It's possible I'll write it that way."

"Not definite?"

"No."

"How cruel you are to a person you love." Her clear, alert eyes warn me not to come out with the cliché that life just happens to be cruel.

Instead I ask, "How many men have you slept with, Christine?"

"With one." I conceal my surprise. "Why do you want to know, Auntie? Has Mum commissioned you to worm it out of me?"

"In that case I would not have asked."

She gives me one of her charming, little-girl smiles. "So you're asking of your own accord. Are you checking out the statistics? Were you thinking of using me as a model for your princess, or are you worrying about me the way Mum does?"

"It's a matter of pure curiosity."

"Mum does it constantly. Worries, I mean. She likes Frank, and she knows we are living together. She doesn't even make a fuss when I am visiting her in Bochum and Frank happens to be in town and I don't come home at night, but the next morning I find her moping around with her eyes all red. That's silly."

"So you find it silly when a person's eyes are all red from crying?"

She does not reply. After a while: "No, of course

27

not. But why does she do everything she can to make me feel guilty?''

It would be of no help to either Christine or me if I said that most mothers, my own included, evoke guilt in their daughters. So I say nothing. Eager to be helpful, but at a loss.

''I was hoping you would say something to Mum. She's so fond of you.'' So she wants me to speak to her mother. Surely she does not have a letter in mind. Nowadays people call each other up. I too use the telephone. Another addiction. I try to pay no attention to the telephone bill, which is paid automatically out of my bank account, and usually I succeed. I ask the usual questions: How are you, what kind of weather are you having, when are we going to see each other? I use these trivia to coax a familiar voice into my living room. A rabbit conjured out of a top hat.

So this evening I shall pick up the receiver, with one of my hearing aids switched to its induction mode, which unscrambles the mechanically amplified sound, and say: Christine was here to see me. Yes, today. She's a bit upset with you. Why? She feels you are putting pressure on her. You don't see how she can feel that way when you give her complete freedom? It's true, you do, but you never let her forget how difficult it is for you. Oh, you say you make such an effort not to let her notice? But she senses the effort, you can be sure of that, and it oppresses her. What do *I* think you should do? You should try to give her real freedom, with conviction. Where do you find conviction? Let yourself fall in love again. No, I have not gone out of my mind. You're not too old. Let it happen, and you'll see how well you and Christine get along.

But of course the conversation will be entirely

different—more painful, more dishonest on both sides. And nothing will have been accomplished.

"Let your mother worry about you a little."

Christine frowns. "She says she lives only for me. That's ridiculous. She should live for herself. I'm fond of her, but this is impossible."

She is right. She is wrong. I talk to Christine about her mother, trying to explain something that can hardly be explained in words. It was shortly after the war that I made the acquaintance of her mother, a young actress whom I had first seen in *Mourning Becomes Electra*. She was in mourning not only for O'Neill's afflicted family but also for Germany. She felt guilty, even though she had been little more than a child when the Nazis came to power, and sprang from a family that had hated Hitler. She wanted to do penance, do penance to me because I was Jewish. I frustrated her because I was looking for friendship, not acts of penance. I could not conceive what she meant by that nebulous concept. Certainly nothing religious—God seemed not to enter the picture. If indeed she had ever counted on God, she now felt utterly abandoned. She wanted to serve me. I hurt her by not cooperating. By giving her no opportunity to relieve her compulsion to do good works. She went off in search of other objects for her pity and found the most unsuitable one of all: mankind. She and her husband grew apart. She had met him during the war; she was close to the resistance movement known as the Kreisau Circle and had to go into hiding after the July 20 attempt at assassinating Hitler. She married him, the resistance hero, after the war, without noticing that his political commitment had evaporated. He became a lawyer, and things went well for him in our spanking-new, richly blessed democracy. He was successful, joined the Christian Democratic

Party and the Rotary Club, and played golf. "When your parents separated, your mother had long since given up her profession and did not know how to get back in. She remained alone. All she had was you and her various charities. That is why she turned into the person she is, a disappointed, weary, sometimes overwrought woman."

"Oh, you and your psychological explanations," Christine says, unconvinced.

My automatic hospitality-reflexes come into play. "Would you like a cup of coffee?"

"No thanks."

"Something to eat?"

"No thanks."

"A drink?"

After a moment's hesitation, "That would be nice."

"Whiskey, brandy, sherry?"

"A whiskey soda."

I go into the kitchen to fix her drink. Drop two ice cubes into the glass. "Aren't you having anything, Auntie?" she asks when I come back into the room.

"Not this early in the day."

"As a matter of principle?"

"No, I just don't feel like it."

"That's better." She looks at me intently. Then she suddenly says kindly, "You should get yourself another dog."

"Absolutely not."

"Why not?"

"I'm too old."

"That doesn't make any sense. Being old shouldn't stop you from having a dog."

"Just figure it out: by the time a young dog reaches twelve or fourteen . . ."

"You might be dead. Or sick. Frank and I love dogs. We could take it."

"I'll give it some thought."

A pause. "Was it very hard on you this time?"

"Yes, it was."

"Worse than with any other dog you had?"

"Much worse." I always knew what a danger a dog constituted for me—any stranger the animal annoyed might simply do away with it. If I wished to preserve my sanity, I could not allow myself to love anything that could be killed. And yet I did. I loved Urs, and things went fairly well; he died a natural death, and I had no need to take leave of my senses. It was not anyone's cruelty, or my own negligence, that caused his bone marrow to be flooded with bad cells until it could no longer produce any blood. But a dog. So vulnerable, so out of place in a world dominated by technology.

When he did not return that evening, I knew he never would, but there was still an element of uncertainty because I had not seen him dead. For weeks I slept with the doors open at night, for fear I might not hear his barking. I advertised in the paper, promising a large reward. Countless times I received telephone calls from people who said there was a new dog in their neighborhood who barked all night, and their neighbors were perfectly capable of stealing a dog. A hound, yes, dark brown with white markings, with a bushy tail, yes, of medium size, exactly; they hadn't been able to see whether he had a collar on, but there was no doubt it was mine, and I should on no account mention who had called. The reward? We could discuss that later, that was not why they had called, they only wanted to help. Of course I drove out there, following directions often so vague I had to keep asking. I would find myself standing by an enclosure where an unknown dog barked at me; or would wait a long time until someone came out of the house leading a dog on a leash—a St. Bernard, a poodle, a mongrel, or sometimes a hound of the sort one often sees in the Ticino, white with yellow spots. Many doggy eyes gazed at me amiably, fiercely, pleadingly, until I turned and fled back to my car, where I broke down and sobbed. I leaned back against the upholstery he had gnawed, but even the frayed leather did not remind me how much trouble he had caused me. I had completely forgotten how easily a dog can be replaced. It was no animal I was mourning for. In my poor head he grew and grew, would no longer fit into my room, into my house, and then with his terrible size he battered down all the walls I had painstakingly erected around myself in the course of the last forty years to enable me to live.

I regret, profoundly regret that I am still alive, and do not understand how it is possible. I have loved and flirted, formed friendships and enjoyed them to the utmost, I have written a couple of books, although I do not take them as seriously as I meant to when I still believed that every survivor had the obligation to bear witness. But when my dog disappeared, I began to brood on all the conceivable forms of slaughter, and now I ask myself time and time again what sort of a person I am that I can live with Waiki's murder.

"Why didn't you people resist?" Christine asks. What made her think of that? What were we discussing? It sometimes happens nowadays that I find myself in the middle of a situation without being able to reconstruct how I got into it. But perhaps Christine did not even ask that question, and I am only imagining that she did because I know that her generation asks it, indignantly and angrily.

I do not answer her. We look at each other in silence. A wave of tenderness sweeps through me. I cannot give her an answer, do not even know the answer. I cannot retrace my steps to a time when I had never heard of genocide, when the technology of destruction was foreign to me, when I could so underestimate the extent of the Germans' dehumanization as to say, "Adults, perhaps, but they would never kill innocent children."

Why did we offer no resistance? I cannot recall how it felt not even to suspect that the decision had been made to eliminate us.

"What's wrong?" Christine asks.

"Oh, nothing."

"Your dog's death opened up an old wound, didn't it?"

"Yes."

"The trauma caused by the persecution?"

"Yes."

And now the question comes again, stern and demanding: "Why didn't you people resist?"

I pour myself a brandy and gulp it down. How can anyone be expected to explain human behavior, which was, is, and will remain irrational? The best I can do is try to describe specific situations: "It began quite gradually. We had already experienced it in Germany and again in Holland. First Jews were banned from civil service jobs, then they were forbidden to use the streetcar, the public baths, benches in the parks. Then they could not leave Amsterdam, or go to the movies and the theater. We were allowed to shop only between three and five o'clock, our telephones were taken away, and our radios. We had to register, to report all our holdings, our household goods. Then came the star. We were marked, outlaws, branded for destruction. By then you were reduced to thinking only of yourself, hunting for the gap in the net through which you might slip. There were not many gaps, but there were a few; the net had been knotted by too many hands, and there was no one who had a complete overview. There were almost 130,000 of us Jews—130,000 terrified individuals, not one group, at best grouplets, many of the Jews assimilated, quite a number of them baptized, a number of them orthodox. There were capitalists and proletarians, Dutch Jews, German and Polish Jews, and the Nazis split our ranks still further by granting dispensations to metal workers, diamond cutters, veterans of front-line combat in World War I, members of the Jewish Council, leading manufacturers, scientists, artists. Then they canceled the dispensations and hauled us away street by street, or according to the first letter of our last names, or according to profession. I do not know whether this was a deliberate tactic; I suspect it was more a matter of intuition on their part: This is how to prevent resistance from arising. Play off one against the other, so that no sense of solidarity can form.''

Christine shakes her head, whether at the Nazis or at our passivity I do not know. At any rate, I sense her scorn. Yet after a while she hugs me, kisses me, and says with a reflective smile, ''And now you are writing a book about a girl who did resist.'' She looks at her watch. ''Auntie, I have to be going.'' And as she kisses me again in parting, she says cheerfully, ''But you must tell me about what went on with that shepherd.''

3

Back to the sofa. Exhausted from coping with that little blond witch, and feeling at once happy and miserable. By now my established pattern for dealing with others: first I long for them to come, then I wish they were gone.

Come ye and admire me. Tell me how impressed you are. You often say that. I enjoy hearing it, and trot around the ring to resounding applause, a circus horse who covers her wound with sequins, concealing, suppressing, pretending. In reality I simply allow myself to drift in the current of least resistance. If nothing but a green apple is available, I do not ask for a red one, and if no apple is to be had, I do without. It took me quite a while to attain this degree of equanimity. When I was younger, I would set my heart on getting what I wanted. I rushed in hot pursuit of goals without having the faintest idea of where they might be found or whether they even existed. Now I pursue nothing at all; instead, I crouch on the ground and creep about, always in a circle.

Come ye and admire me. My tolerance (worth mentioning only to a believer), my independence (outward independence—what sort of accomplishment is that when you have money? inner independence—the work of a lifetime, never completed), hunted and snared, yet not to be done in. Dead of an abortion (at age twenty), an overdose of sleeping pills (at age twenty-four), murdered in a concentration camp (at age thirty-five), and still here.

Come ye and do not admire me: Tell me the truth. A woman who cannot jump over the shadow of her own origins, who rejects herself and flails about. A distraught woman, who does not draw the proper conclusions.

Do not come, leave me alone. Let me have my solitude, do not force me to join in your stupid game.

This constant dwelling on what lies ahead. The gradual waning of my powers. No longer wanted. No longer being part of things. Losing my imposing appearance, my beauty, my sparkle. Of all the forms of humanity, I have always found old women the most repulsive. The stench of centuries of subjugation clings to us. Mixed with the musty odor of bourgeois stuffiness. Oppressed and pampered. Kept away from the earth, that source of strength our feet never touched. To be sure, there are also matriarchal heroines and Indian squaws with their bold, masculine faces, Tahitian women who wear their muumuus like royal purple robes, Italian nonnas full of dignity in their eternal widow's weeds.

My grandmother, always in black, buttoned up to the neck—about fifty when my earliest memories of her begin, at that time not yet widowed and condemned to sackcloth and ashes, praised by all for the smartness of her dress—she had a smell that made me gag. I spent countless hours in school brooding about how I might best do away with her. That was hate, real hate.

Am I to blame for being betrayed and abandoned? Betrayed by whom? There would have had to be someone who had formed an alliance with me and then broken it. There is no such person. Cannot be.

Only young people can enter into alliances. But there I go again, overrating youth. As if you could overrate it. And yet I have not forgotten how terrible it is to be young. A permanent state of insanity, which in retrospect one considers happiness.

Antigone is young. Young above all else. No matter what doubts are raised about her conduct, her youth cannot be questioned. Love is not off limits to her. It can be a shepherd, a prince, a god. The love story, invented in the days when I would say "Greece" without having been there and actually mean "the South." Synonyms for the South: home, sorrow, harshness, silence, heat, midday, cliffs with scrub vegetation, the smell of the macchia, the sea lapping the shore, emerald green along the edge, black above the seaweed-covered rocks, blending into its real, unbelievable color, that blue somewhat lighter than violets and somewhat darker than the sky. The most beautiful thing in the world. At that time the South to me meant Positano, where rosemary, myrtle, lavender, broom, and tiger lilies bloomed. It is into this landscape that I transpose Antigone whenever I am swept with compassion at the thought that she is to die without having known love. *Oedipus at Colonnus*

She wanders through the mountains with the blind man. His guide, his provider. She quickly learned that one need not starve, even if there are no servants to bring food on golden platters. She became independent, clever, resourceful.

A few days of rest in an abandoned cottage. Her father is not feeling well and lies there, listlessly waving off the flies.

"Don't hover over me," he says feebly. "Make

37

yourself useful, or lie down under a tree and sleep. Leave me in peace."

There is no tree outside. Only a steep slope covered with scrub vegetation. Broom, rosemary, thyme. Intoxicating scents. Might there be ripe berries higher up?

A few steps up the hillside. Suddenly a hissing. A viper rears up, its forked tongue darting menacingly.

A stone whistles through the air. Strikes the snake square on the head, smashing it. The creature lies dead on the ground, a small, twisted, spotted branch. Only a god would have such good aim. A god slew the snake.

Her knees give way. As she falls, a ledge grazes her skin. A little blood. Her eyes close and open again. A man with a slingshot in his hand comes running down the slope. A man—no, a god. The god who struck down the snake.

He kneels beside her, is muscular and smooth-skinned, with the broad brow of a lion, a short, straight nose, and full lips.

His mouth comes close, sucks in hers—it is not a kiss but a bite, his tongue between her teeth, nausea, choking. Suddenly fear: a murderer, he is a murderer. Pounding his chest with her fists. Kicking. Then falling, falling into his arms. Joining into his game with the tongue.

He lets go. A deep breath and another embrace. Melting away, drowning.

He smells, the immortal one, of goat stall and warm human skin. Not repulsive, no, exciting, tender—it makes her laugh and cry. Between kisses he whispers, "My princess." He knows who she is; that is all right, saves explanations.

His name? He must have a name, after all. There is no god without a name. Who can it be? He is not powerful enough for Zeus, not graceful enough for Hermes. Hephaestus or Ares? Too alien, too distant. Poseidon? Unthinkable in the mountains. The only two left are Apollo and Dionysus. Apollo? This man with the short nose is not beautiful, not fair enough. Then she notices his water skin, with a blooming pomegranate twig sticking out of it. So he is Dionysus. Her cousin seven times removed, come into the world out of the fire that consumed his mother, drawn by Zeus from the flames, the god born of death, the god of intoxication, suffering, and dying.

Swooped up in his arms, her face pressed to his chest. Floating, flying up the slope and gently sinking down into the straw in a sooty stable.

"Hungry?"

"No."

"Thirsty?"

"No."

"Tired?"

"No."

He laughs, takes a clay jug and goes outside. Alone, she listens, tense and excited, holding her breath until he returns, a white cloth around his loins, droplets of water glistening on his skin. He unties the cloth, comes closer, dark and naked, grows out of the earth, a giant, a lion about to pounce, a dense cloud that descends on her.

That is how it was. The first time. The beginning. Life. There is a buzzing in my head. I have been lying on the sofa too long. I get up and go to my desk.

4

There on my desk is the telephone. My notebook. Should I write? Should I make a telephone call? Lie down? Go for a walk? Read? Listen to music? The hard part if you live alone and practice a profession: you can do anything you like. Limitless possibilities. Constant indecision. I wait. I do not know what for. No, I do know, but . . . Am I losing my senses?

A glance at the telephone, which does not ring. Why no call from him? He used to call so often. Every day when we were separated. Sometimes twice in one day. To tell me he was going out to lunch now. That lunch was over, and what he had ordered. That it was raining in the city where he happened to be. That the sun was shining. That he had bought himself a pair of shoes, black or brown. That he had just seen a stimulating television program. That a good program was on, and I should watch it. That he was enjoying a book. That the rehearsal had not gone well. That the German theater as a whole was not worth a damn, especially the opera. That only a madman would want to be a director. And at the end, as always: How's your old pal? Give him a kiss on the nose for me.

If he called, I would have to say: I let the dog run away. Toward evening, you know, when I always let him out. He didn't come back. Of course I looked for him. For days. For weeks. Even though I was sure the very first night that he was dead. Just as dead as you, Urs, or almost. Let's give his life a whisper of a chance. You don't have that. I saw you dead, even if I barely looked. I signed a paper saying I agreed to your cremation. In my desk is the notification that the urn with your ashes was buried as per my instructions in that grave I do not visit. Total cost, including coffin, cremation, urn, transportation: 1525.50 marks. I allowed them to burn your "mortal remains." As if I believed in immortality. I agreed to your being shoved into the oven like a log.

Once again I was alone. Drained by your long illness. Eight months of lies: The doctor is very pleased, in six months at most you'll be well again, as well as before, and next fall we'll take that trip to Turkey. You want to see Malta? Of course, Malta is fine with me. Four times a day the route from the hospital entrance to your room, three hundred twenty-five interminable steps, the gloomy, buff-colored enamel on the walls, with lighter patches, as if something had been hastily painted over, perhaps murals from the Nazi period. Then your optimism, your will to live, your difficult death.

Everyone assures me it was a gentle death. Which is true, if one thinks of the final twelve hours, not true if one thinks of the last months. For the nineteen-year-old girl, in the room next to yours for a week, who suffocates and hemorrhages to death the night you die, the death struggle is certainly worse. The nurses are crying as they come out of her room; a new experience, seeing nurses actually cry. The entire ward—the head doctor's private ward with thirteen beds, whose sheltering perfection has imprisoned us for months—is in an uproar. To be sure, even in this crisis no one goes so far as to speak the forbidden word *leukemia*, even though it is on everyone's mind here. But the terrible dying, of which I see only the blood-drenched sheets that are whisked out of the room, disrupts the routine. And still the doctors are not willing to take action. The Hippocratic oath. Dedicated to healing. Keep the body alive at all costs. Binding orders. But even if anyone wanted to do something, he would be prevented by the dying girl's mother. A plump woman, her eyes red from weeping, she flits back and forth between the room and the corridor, ringing her hands—the first time I have actually seen a person ring her hands—and repeating in a shrill voice to the very end, "You keep on hoping, keep on hoping." The father sits silently for seven days and nights at a little round table in the corridor. His well-pressed suit gradually becomes more and more wrinkled and soiled. Only when the call-light over his daughter's door goes on does he put aside his book, a volume bound in red leather with gilt ornamentation, which he is reading or not reading, and tiptoe in to his daughter. We argue politely about whether the death of a nineteen-year-old is worse than that of a sixty-year-old; I assert that it is, while he denies it. Once, when he has closed the door behind him I glance out of curiosity at his book. It is *The Brothers Karamazov*, opened to the part where Ivan describes children being tortured. From then on I check every day—the book is always open to the same passage; perhaps he is trying to take comfort in the thought that torture inflicted by human beings is worse than the torture inflicted by an illness.

We think along the same lines, are seeking the same kind of support. My wound bleeds when anyone touches it and sometimes when it is not touched, unexpectedly, unpredictably, when I am swimming in the Mediterranean, discussing an entirely different subject, walking through a city, making love. The wound is there, but sometimes weeks, months, even years pass during which I hardly feel it. I do not wait for Waiki's phone call, cannot even remember whether I ever spoke to him on the telephone. Probably often; perhaps my heart pounded when I heard his voice, which I loved but can no longer recall; perhaps I kissed the receiver out of which it came, perhaps I stayed home for days on end so as not to miss his call—I simply do not remember. Forty years are long, forty years of death cannot be bridged.

If Urs called up now, what would he say about my dog? He who fussed over every little thing, who blamed me for bad weather, a botched performance, a missed rendezvous, was tender and understanding whenever things got serious. He would say: It wasn't your fault; the dog had a good life, we'll get another one; you'll see how soon he takes the place of the lost one. He does not say it, does not call, and I must come to terms with my dog's death on my own. Urs was a master at fudging his way through life; he fudged his way through his career, through friendships and loves, and with his complaining and cursing and occasional faking still managed to get what he wanted. I fudged right along with him, not quite so expertly, but deriving a certain pleasure from it. Since Urs has been gone there has been no more fudging, and I have lost the knack.

He does not call. I give up, stifle the desire to lie down again, pick up the newspaper once more, and manage to find something I had overlooked before. A piece of news that concerns me. That no longer concerns me, but which affects me as though it did: retired undersecretary of state Dr. Ludwig Haverkamp has died of a heart attack at the age of seventy-two. When I met him, fours years of war still stood between him and his career in the Federal Republic of Germany, nor do I know whether his ascent began immediately in 1945 or whether he first had to wend his way though the tangle of denazification. He was beyond any doubt a fellow traveler, with or without Party insignia. The administrator placed in charge of Jewish businesses in Holland, with a fancy office in The Hague. The administrator of Waiki's little pharmaceutical company; once he took over, Waiki was out. "This man Haverkamp—" he spluttered in a rage, then tried to smile. "A perfectly nice fellow, actually—in any other situation."

A few weeks later Waiki is arrested. Seized in the course of a punitive operation. A so-called punitive operation. Allegedly a bomb went off in a house occupied by German soldiers. Perhaps it was not a bomb at all. There was talk of drunk Germans playing with hand grenades. Perhaps someone just farted. Later on it would take even less than a German fart to set in motion the murder of Jews. During this raid— the second in Amsterdam—three hundred Jewish men under thirty are supposed to be arrested on the basis of previously prepared lists. But since orders call for the entire thing to be over in two hours, a number of older men whose names do not appear on the lists are arrested. Waiki is thirty-two.

For ten days he is interned in a Dutch camp; for ten days there is hope of getting him out. The only person I can turn to is Haverkamp. I try to persuade him to go to the Gestapo and pound the table— pounding the table seems to be the most obvious and the only effective argument—because he needs Waiki during the takeover of the company. Actually a perfectly nice person, toward me as well: genial, suave, skilled at dealing with people. "I assure you, madam, I find my work here far from pleasant, but in wartime everyone must remain at the post to which he has been assigned." If I were not Jewish, he would probably have said, "In the Fatherland's hour of need." "My dear lady, I understand your sense of despair" —he does not understand in the slightest, not in the slightest—"but you must adjust to the idea that your husband will be treated as an enemy alien and kept interned for the duration of the war." *Interned*, he says; *enemy alien; for the duration of the war.*

"He is not interned, he is not an enemy alien but a German Jew, who will be deported to a concentration camp and killed."

"But, my dear lady, you cannot seriously believe that. A person who by a regrettable coincidence got himself into a difficult position has been arrested as a hostage, as it were, for certain attacks against Germans. Obviously he is known not to have been personally involved."

"He is a Jew."

"That complicates the situation, of course. I already said: internment until the end of the war. Certainly not pleasant, but still better than having to face enemy fire on the battlefront. And please do not believe all those tales you hear about a person's being killed merely for being a Jew."

I must not cry, otherwise he will think I am hysterical and will do nothing for me. I keep talking, trying to control my voice, hearing it tremble, go hoarse, begin to croak. He raises his eyebrows, but he remains patient, does not throw me out, listens to me for two whole hours; nothing forces him to do that, certainly not compassion; most likely his upbringing obliges him to address me as "my dear lady," in a kind of social solidarity that is more than skin-deep and remains in effect long after we have been utterly degraded and branded. Not until they shave our

46

heads and drive us naked into the gas chambers will it cease to function. Several times he repeats the phrases "internment, of the sort we had between 1914 and 1918," and "such a sensitive, intelligent person, whom I developed tremendous respect for, even during our short acquaintance," and "until the end of the war." Suddenly he smiles: "I believe you will not have long to wait, my dear lady. You will soon have your husband back. It looks as though our troops are rolling right along in Russia. This will not be a drawn-out war." The German–Russian conflict has been going on for a week. Haverkamp seems very sure of his prediction. In his glee, he forgets who I am. Or does he fail to realize that a German victory will mean not only Waiki's death but my own as well?

Do I realize that myself? As if in a trance I speak the sentence I have probably never formulated for myself with such clarity: "They will kill not only him but all of us. All the Jews." He is pulled up short for a moment, then takes my hands with a laugh. "Dear child"—*my dear lady* sticks in his throat now, but *dear child* is a diminutive form of it—"what an absurd idea. Such a little scaredy-cat." He pens a few lines to the Gestapo, to the effect that his work would be greatly facilitated if he could consult Waiki on a number of points. The coward! Of course that will not be enough. I leave, aware that I have lost the most crucial conversation of my life. My gift for making things clear with words is in tatters. I will not write another line.

Now Haverkamp is dead. His heart could not hold out any longer, his well-bred heart, shielded from the misery of others by cool rationality. Mevrouw De Gruyter, Waiki's secretary, told me that when the news of Waiki's death arrived three months later, Haverkamp was "extremely upset" and expressed his "deepest regret." Clichés. Perhaps at this very moment someone is uttering the same clichés at his graveside. Waiki's murder, old Haverkamp's failed heart—lumped into the same category by the abuse of language.

I wonder whether he ever thought about me again? About Waiki, whom he could have saved? Whether he shuddered every time or even only once at the mention of a concentration camp. After the war he doubtless would have been proud to be able to say he had saved a Jew's life. But since he had no such tale to tell, he probably dismissed the whole business with the convenient assertion, "As an individual you were helpless." And it was not just the business with Waiki and me he dismissed, but anything that might have prevented him from speaking the beloved word *Germany* with untainted pleasure. It is true that the individual was helpless. It was not true. For instance, he, Haverkamp, could have done something. So long as Waiki was still in Holland. After that, no.

Perhaps it would have been better if I had given in to hysteria. Perhaps my hysteria would have affected him. Perhaps that was the only way to crack his shell of propriety and timidity. In his position Haverkamp would have needed only a speck of courage to go to the Gestapo. Some of those arrested with Waiki were freed. Two who were asked for more insistently by the Germans administering their firms, a few who were ill, a few about whose rescue nothing leaked out, the sons of very rich parents. He did not have the courage, that tiny speck of courage; Germans too were terrified of the Gestapo. The only risk he ran was that an SS officer—someone of Haverkamp's sort never dealt with subordinates—might note mentally, or at worst on paper: *Intercedes for Jews.* This missing speck of courage was responsible for Waiki's not being rescued from a horrible death, and for my wound which will never heal.

5

The telephone rings. I allow myself to think it is Urs, pretend I think it is, as I sometimes pretend that I open the door and Waiki is standing outside. I clumsily adjust my hearing aid and pick up the receiver. In my agitation I cannot even manage to say hello. I hear my own breath, or someone else's. Finally a man's voice says impatiently, "With whom am I speaking, please?" Herr Schieding, my tax consultant. I whisper, "Hello." His tone promptly turns friendly. He says something must be wrong with my telephone or with his—he simply could not hear me. He just wants to ask whether he may drop by this afternoon; my tax return is finished and he needs my signature; no, he prefers not to send the return through the mails. There are a few things to discuss, not directly connected with the return; but he wants to talk to me about my securities.

All right. Let him come. After four. That anal-retentive fussbudget. I dislike him because he forces me to pay attention to things I find unpleasant. Because he never stops blithering on about money—investing money, earning money, making money grow.

My ambivalence toward all this. Aside from the five years in Holland when I worked as a photographer, I never had a proper profession. I did many things, but never under the pressure of it's-this-or-starve. First my father provided for me, then Waiki, then Waiki's factory, then Urs. I never did quite understand how people went about accumulating money. Only when my very survival was at stake did I do as others do, amazed to discover that it actually worked.

After the war I had no fonder wish than to do some writing at long last. But I was practical enough to realize I needed a source of support first. I salvaged what could be salvaged of Waiki's pharmaceutical company. First in Holland, where with the help of two employees I did everything: typed letters, sterilized bottles and filled them, procured raw materials, designed brochures, called on physicians with samples. Then in Germany. Here, more was on the line. I negotiated with the people who had once pressured us into selling out at a ridiculous price. When forced to return the company, they urged me to merge with their own much larger concern. I did not want a merger. I was acting not only on my own behalf but also for Waiki's mother and brother in America. That was enough to keep me from caving in. I stood fast and got my way. Only after that did I begin to write, but I also translated novels from English and Dutch. Composed the scripts for documentaries, reviewed books on the radio. But when I wanted to travel, I traveled, when I wanted to see friends, I saw them, and when I wanted to read, I read. I let myself be seduced by whatever gave me pleasure. But why am I thinking of my susceptibility to seduction in the past tense? As if things were any different now. As if my age prevented me from running after anything that promises diversion, variety, involvement. As if I did not do exactly what appeals to me at any given moment. As if I did not worry that my Antigone book, which means more to me than anything else, may never be finished.

My princess. A beautiful artistic creation that at many moments—but not all—fulfills my expectations as well as I could wish. Who can be sent away and summoned at will. Who does not destroy my solitude but makes it more lucid. My relationship to her: the eroticism of solitude.

From early childhood on. Her longing for solitude, and mine. She in a palace, I in an upper-middle-class villa, both of us surrounded by many people, pampered, loved—and yet . . . Aloneness as a character trait. Living inwardly. Living for oneself. Seeking contact with others, but unwilling to relinquish secrets. Even to much-loved brothers. To them least of all.

I brood a good deal about our families. In the vague hope of finding similarities.

We are both daddy's girls. Showered with love and understanding. My father liked to say, ''Parents exist for their children, not the reverse,'' and he acted accordingly. He did not prohibit and he did not punish. When I was six he would read aloud to me in bed on Sunday mornings: the fable of Reynard the Fox, Goethe's *Hermann and Dorothea*, an idyll in hexameters, Schiller's *Mary Stuart*. When I was twelve we read *Faust*, dividing up the parts between us. I climbed my first mountain with him, he took me to the opera—we sat in the middle of the front row, right behind the conductor; and later, when I came home from the university for vacation, he met me at the railway station, a red rose in his hand. His tender solicitude gave me strength enough to last a lifetime; I have survived and grown old, as old as he was when he died—''just in the nick of time,'' that is, still at home in Germany. I have managed to stay on course, while maintaining both sides of a double life, a proper bourgeois and a naughty bohemian, keeping the two as far apart as possible.

Oedipus, a good king, not a strong one, amiable, cheerful, and serene until the hour of truth, when everything collapsed and he gouged out his eyes in order to see no more. Then dependent on the help of strangers, cared for by Antigone. She assumed the role of nurse, servant, and companion; one may at least suspect that his feelings for her were something more than fatherly.

My mother—everyone called her Aunt Mara, whether they knew her very well or only slightly—small, agile, blond and blue-eyed, almost always in a classic tailored suit with a white blouse, never at a loss, witty, willing to put her hand in the fire for others, but not willing to hold her tongue. She always expressed her opinion with brutal frankness; in a very bourgeois world she was very unbourgeois, and enjoyed being different: a snob who exerted the same attraction on aristocrats, artists, and people with botched lives. She loved to play matchmaker, and her indiscretions ofter produced confusion, but confusion was her element. My friends adored her, and the less they themselves conformed to society's expectations, the more they worshiped her. Pampered and oppressed by her, I used to think enviously: How well I would get along with her if only she were not my mother.

And Jocasta? Why does she remain so shadowy? She is always referred to as if she were somehow a secondary character, someone who merely gave the cue for the others' grand tragedy. As if it were scarcely worthwhile to pay much attention to her. Oedipus—now there is a rewarding figure! He killed his father and married his mother. When a son marries his mother, the mother is also marrying her son, yet the oracle that predicted this misfortune was concerned solely with him. Even in that first oracle that warned Laius he would die at the hand of his own son, not a word was said about Jocasta, unless one considers her included in the grim prophecy that stated the entire family would perish through the fault of a child not yet conceived. Sometimes the struggle between Creon and Antigone is interpreted as a confrontation between patriarchy and matriarchy. If that is correct, Jocasta uncomplainingly accepted the passive female role. She killed no one but herself. She does fulfill certain dramatic functions. One of them is to bring Creon into the story. He intervenes in the action because he is her brother.

Sister, spouse, mother—what more can one want? So much material on a woman, yet not enough to lend her substance. No psychological complex has been named after her. We must assume she loved Laius; otherwise, she would hardly have consented to having her son exposed. Or if not consented, at least not resisted. But perhaps she did not wish to have a son by a man she hated. The sources say nothing of how she behaved when the child was taken away. A baffling mother. A no less baffling wife. Laius had abducted young Prince Chrysippus, and Euripides calls him the inventor of pederasty. Was that what she was after? And if so, why? Many interpretations suggest themselves. Perhaps she yearned for humiliation, or simply wanted to be left in peace; perhaps she used Laius as a shield behind which she disported with other men, or else she carried on with his boys, by herself or together with him, or the relationship between a man and a boy was arousing to her, or she loved women, or she could derive happiness from the sensitive understanding of a homosexual. But if one of these possibilities is true, or all of them, what was her relationship to Oedipus? Did she love him? Only because he looked like Laius? Had she grown indifferent toward herself as she aged? Perhaps it made her feel good to be desired by a man so much younger. But did he in fact desire her? After all, this marriage was not a matter of passion; no Oedipus complex drove them into each other's arms. To be sure, the young prince actually killed the man who had begotten him and married the woman who had given birth to him. Two strangers. He had grown up at the court of Corinth. His father was called King Polybus, his mother Queen Merope. His desire for Jocasta did not result from those dark urges that bind a little son to his mother; he married her as an adjunct to a kingdom; both together had been the prize promised by Creon to whoever vanquished the Sphinx.

Apparently Oedipus thought nothing of marrying a woman so much older than he. In Greece such things were not considered important. Perhaps she said coquettishly on their wedding night: You are so young, Oedipus. I could almost be your mother. And he, who certainly did not like to hear the word *mother* in connection with his wife, would have taken her quickly in his arms and replied: Do not make much of the few years' advantage you may have over me. She did not discover the scars on his ankles. Or if she did discover them, she did not associate them with anything in particular. (Possibly she did not know the holes had been pierced in the child's ankles when he was exposed.) She was not pulled up short by the odd name "Swollen Foot"—she thought it was a common name in Corinth.

She bore him four children. Four children to take the place of the one who was no longer there. (It may be that the child she had abandoned occasionally appeared to her in dreams, a helpless newborn or a monster that seized her in its claws and demanded love.) Two sons, two daughters. It is not recorded whether she preferred the boys to the girls, or whether she got along better with the two uncomplicated ones—with Eteocles, stalwart and stupid as heroes tend to be, and pale Ismene—or with the difficult ones, Polyneices and Antigone.

We may assume that at the side of her youthful husband she fought a hard battle to preserve her beauty, and relied more than usual on the skills of masseurs, bath attendants, cosmetics specialists, and doctors. It is possible that she took to her bed for a day or two every four weeks, feigning an indisposition that had long since ceased. The women of her own age must have whispered and giggled; Oedipus, blind long before he actually blinded himself, noticed nothing.

Not so Antigone and Polyneices. They would meet in the olive grove outside the South Gate. There they would lie side by side in the moss, putting together clues without knowing where they would lead.

He: Mother is putting on an act.

She: Mothing is hiding something. Something must have happened back when she was still married to Grandfather Laius.

He: Grandfather?

She: That's what we always used to call him.

He: That was when we were little. I don't like that anymore. He wasn't our grandfather.

She: She says we look like him.

He: One of her crazy notions.

She: You don't want to look like anyone.

He: No.

She: Because you want the world to begin with you.

He: With the two of us.

I lie next to my big brother in the pine grove of our parents' grounds. We have taken refuge here because company is coming, people we dislike. He tells me about a girl he is in love with. "Do you expect you two will get married?"

"Yes, I think so." He says it so calmly, as if it were the most natural thing in the world that he should leave me. And in fact it is the most natural thing. Do I really believe that my brother, twelve years older than I, will always live at home, travel with me, go skiing and mountain-climbing with me, take me to the theater, to call on people, where we sit in a corner and make fun of the other guests? Do I really believe he is as passionate about being a brother as I am about being a sister?

In this hour, when the pain of parting overcomes me, I am molded once and for all by my love for him.

It is myself in my role as sister who gazes at me out of my golden mirror.

6

I am hungry again. Since my ulcer ten years ago I feel the need to eat every two or three hours. With neither schedule nor self-control, sometimes too much, sometimes too little; when I am alone I never sit down to a proper cooked meal—I just snack, on sweet things and sour things and then sweet things again; my stomach can tolerate anything but emptiness. Almost every day I go downstairs to the store on the ground floor of my building and select some groceries. Occasionally a fat woman or a compulsive talker blocks the aisle, and I am seized with claustrophobia. Then I stuff into my wire basket whatever comes to hand. My favorite food is caviar on hot buttered toast. But for caviar I would have to go into town; my grocer does not stock it. That in itself would not deter me, nor would the price; for I do not pinch pennies. If I do not eat caviar, it is only because I have a foolish aversion to eating it all by myself.

In my earlier days it would never have occurred to me to think about food unless it was to be shared. Except for that last winter of the war, when I was in hiding in Amsterdam, itself cut off from the world, and could think of little but food. An instructive experience: to discover how hunger can torment you, although many who made the same discovery at the time now act as if they knew nothing about it and frequently voice the opinion that the wretched of this earth, hopelessly preoccupied with a crust of bread, a tortilla, a handful of rice, are stupid, untalented, incapable of development.

What a winter. No electricity, no work, nothing to wait for but the end of the war. One finds it difficult to recall what one is waiting for. After the fall of Paris, the rapid advance of the Allies, the flight of the Dutch Nazis to Germany, the frightful disappointment when the battle for Arnhem is lost and everything comes to a standstill.

This cannot go on for more than a few months, which may be too long for us, but even that does not matter; one accepts the possibility. Hunger, cold, darkness—the only realities. After one slice of bread for breakfast at nine, I can force myself to concentrate on something else until ten, but from ten to one my thoughts revolve endlessly around the prospect of lunch, two thin slivers of bread with bits of salty fish; we obtained a whole barrel of it in exchange for my pearl necklace. Sometimes there are sugar beets too, cooked in the tin can we use as a stove. The fire under it must be fed constantly with slivers of wood from a door we sawed up.

After the meal I read: books that I, as the offspring of a cultivated family, should have read long ago but did not read because they bored me. Sometimes I did skim a few pages, savoring the style, the story, but for heaven's sake not the whole long-winded thing—and now I wish the books were a great deal longer. I have time, one day passes like the other, and the books provide the only punctuation—one more finished, how long did it take me to read it: two days, a week? Time, of which I have altogether too much, flows by, becomes inconsequential, ceases to be measurable. I read Gottfried Keller's *Green Henry*, Goethe's *Elective*

Affinities and the two volumes of his *Wilhelm Meister*, Jean Paul's *Titan*, many books by Dickens, *Vanity Fair*, *Tristram Shandy*, and *Moby Dick*. I always loved the Russian novelists; now I read them again. Kurt, the "half-Aryan" graphic artist, Waiki's former schoolmate, in whose house I am hidden, has supplemented his own library with those of people in hiding or deported, and it has much to offer, including Shakespeare, without whom I would scarcely have survived the first terrible weeks of being shut in.

By four o'clock, at the latest, I cannot go on reading. The words swim before my eyes. Then comes two hours of thinking intensely about supper—will there be one slice of bread or two? Perhaps as a special treat a couple of tulip bulbs, which are tasty but cause heartburn.

Then the long evening, with political discussions by the light of our single kerosene lamp—kerosene obtained in exchange for phonograph records. When one of us has to go to the bathroom, the others are left sitting in darkness, but even in the darkness Kurt continues with his communist harangues, to which I become increasingly allergic, even though my own views are very far left at the time. Occasionally I argue with him, while his wife maintains a stoic silence. But Kurt is no fun to argue with; he is doctrinaire and self-righteous, and I have to bite my tongue because I am dependent on him. Without electrical current we must do without the great source of comfort we had the previous year, the BBC and Radio Orange broadcasts. Exhausted and depressed, I finally creep into my sleeping place. It is a perfect hideaway. In a small, windowless room set up as a library, one wall of shelving has been shifted a few feet into the room, the ceiling moldings redone to fit the new dimensions of the room; there are two shelves, to which books are glued, that I can remove and replace from the inside. In my little compartment behind the shelves I have food, water, a pail, and a candle. In an emergency I could survive in there for a few days without having to come out. But the emergency never arrives. In the morning I do calisthenics for half an hour, although I know it burns up calories. My fear of getting no exercise is greater than my fear of hunger.

Every few weeks I venture out to see my mother, in hiding with a young couple who live in the country. They are unpleasant people who barely trouble to conceal their anti-Semitism and would make splendid Nazis if they did not think it to their advantage to resist the foreign enemy. The simplest form of resistance: to take in an old Jewish lady who pays well and can be put in charge of the children. On the way I have to pass over a pontoon bridge guarded by German soldiers, older men with tired, morose faces. I pity them because they are in a hostile country, forced to stand around for no good reason. Presumably they pity me, too; I look hungry. We exchange friendly glances. I would like to chat with them, even if only to hear them say they are fed up with the situation. But I dare not—you can never be sure. It is true that no more Jews are being shipped to Poland, but I have no desire to spend the last few weeks of the war under the threat of being shot at any minute. I am also irritated by the Dutch, who look right through the Germans as if they were made of air. I belong to neither group, belong to no one, am alone, without the faintest notion of what to do or where to go once the war is over.

Do I really know what it feels like to be hungry all the time? Like those who have been hungry from generation to generation, whose parents were starving and whose children will starve? I do not. My memories of my own hunger are rather vague. All that remains of it is a myth, the myth into which one stylizes all one's experience and which one reverts to again and again. I was and am privileged, superior to my murderers all the way to the gas chamber.

Can I really imagine the procession to the gas chamber? At the time I thought I could; I followed the poet Rilke's advice to be ahead of every farewell, like the waning winter. I learned his *Sonnets to Orpheus* by heart, so as to have them at my disposal if the book were no longer in my possession. But would I have made use of them? In the face of death would I really have been able to proclaim, "But where there is song, there is Orpheus"? A grotesque notion. I would have trembled like a terrified animal that does not grasp what is happening to it. Shattered, destroyed. As Waiki too was shattered and destroyed. Do not try to weasel your way out; be consistent, face the horrible truth, see how it was, how he suffered, a flayed, hunted creature, think, incessantly think that which cannot be thought to an end.

I am standing in the kitchen with the refrigerator door open as I puzzle over what to eat. I pour myself a glass of milk, put a few chocolate-covered cookies on a plate, carry them into the living room, sit down at the desk, eat and drink. When I am through, I carry the glass and plate back to the kitchen and put them in the sink.

Suddenly I am shivering. The heat is turned off in the kitchen. On my way back into the warm room it occurs to me that I went into the kitchen for a specific reason. I go back, stand by the refrigerator, attempting to reconstruct what I had in mind. I open the door, survey the refrigerator's contents, shift two milk cartons from the middle shelf to the lower one for no particular reason, but I cannot think of anything better to do. Did I mean to eat something? Actually I am full. The refrigerator is well stocked. I am pleased to see all this food—it gives me a sense of security. Like the warm apartment, the full clothes-closet, the car in the garage. Did I want something more to drink? I am not thirsty. What did I want? My glasses? I have them on. My hearing aids? Did I want to get new batteries, which are stored in the refrigerator? But I changed them only yesterday. I slowly turn my head and see the glass and plate in the sink. Feeling depressed, I close the refrigerator door.

Suddenly I am swept by nostalgia for those bygone times when I was in hiding, in fear for my life. When any moment could be the last. Only the faintest chance of surviving. Many threw away that chance by misinterpreting the situation; they thought if they went into hiding and were caught they would be treated as punitive cases. Once in the cattle car they soon enough discovered that there was no distinction between a punitive case and an ordinary Jew. It was always the same gas chamber with the same Cyclone-B. After Waiki's death I knew what was up and was no longer afraid. Nothing worse could happen to me than what had already happened. I wore my composure like a cap of invisibility. It made me invulnerable. My only thought: not to play into the murderer's hands. They wanted to do me in, but for that they first had to have me in their clutches. Therefore: flight. Living on the razor's edge. Survival the only imperative. Nothing else mattered. Survival as a religion. As a sport. As a political ideology. In pitch darkness behind the wall of books, in a hollow compartment just wide enough to let me lie down on a kapok-filled mattress that got more and more matted, under me a clammy sheet, over me a horse blanket. I trembled with cold until sleep came and warmed me.

Living on the razor's edge. O bridal chamber. Abandoned by the gods. Abandoned by everything. Waiting for death.

"If we followed the coast for two or three days, we would come to a mountain range that stretches far out into the sea. In a bay there is a small hidden harbor. High above it are three temples to Hera. Among the rocks grow dwarf firs, battered and twisted by the wind, briars, myrtle, elder. Across the water lies Corinth. In clear weather you can see it."

You can see it. Not he. He is blind, after all.

"You used to go there often?"

"Very often. When there was no wind, the slaves would row me across, and when there was wind, they would set the sails. But my favorite way of getting there was to ride alone by the long land route, crossing the isthmus through the olive groves."

"Why not go there now?"

He draws back his upper lip, grinning, or fighting tears. The face of an old man thinking of his youth. A handsome, creased face. The desire to caress it. But he does not like that. Any show of tenderness must come from him.

"It is not good to visit your own grave. I was happy there."

In earlier times he often spoke of his youth in Corinth. But can you trust your parents' tales? Memories that grow more beautiful with each passing year. How they wish things had been. Only brothers and sisters really know each other. Remember how everything used to be. Oh, Polyneices.

The wind is blowing. The waves have white crests. Lizards scurry over the cliff. The meadows are red with poppies.

Lay aside the net, now repaired. "So we shall stay

here?'' He shakes his head irritably. ''I cannot bear the monotony. Hearing nothing but the sea pounding against the shore. Day in, day out. Smelling nothing but fish and seaweed.''

''You cannot return to Thebes, not so long as Creon is alive. You do not want to go to that mountain range you spoke of. What do you want?''

Tears roll out of the empty sockets and down into his beard. His hand gropes for her. Strokes her. The caress is soothing.

''For us homeless ones one place is like another. We must be thankful if our presence is tolerated. We stay awhile, then we journey on. To the next place, which is strange to us, without memories.'' He withdraws his hand. ''Someday you will return to Thebes. To a town that has changed. You, likewise, are no longer the same as you once were. Each of you will have passed a portion of your history without the other. You no longer match one another perfectly. You will find it difficult to say 'we Thebans.' Perhaps you will say it anyway. Perhaps at certain moments you will feel you are home again. I would wish it for you. But pack up our things now.''

''Where are we going?''

''Through the mountains again. To the Southern Sea. Along its coast toward the sunrise.''

''And then?''

''Do not ask so many questions.'' And with his back to her, ''Then we shall go to Athens.''

Joy, shock. The great city. The hub of the world. With its artists, scholars, philosophers. But the ancient enemy of Thebes.

''Will they take us in, two Thebans?''

''We are exiles. Theseus is a good and intelligent king. I can safely leave you under his protection.''

''Leave me? And what about you?''

He traces a great circle with his right hand. "I shall be everywhere and nowhere. The homeless one returns to the gods. I go to Athens to die."

7

I am reluctant to return to my desk, to the notebook, which challenges and torments me. Instead, I go into the bedroom, where a private staircase leads up to the floor above. The staircase is of wood, painted red, and it is tucked into so small a space that there is barely room to put your left foot on one step, then your right foot on the next. Strangers have a bad time with it, but I am accustomed to it and scramble up nimbly. I emerge from the narrow hatchway into the upper room, which is actually not a room but a wide corridor that goes around two corners, very light and bright. Urs and I threw ourselves into decorating it with great enthusiasm. From this room you have a view of the entire city, now so ugly but from up here quite lovely, the tall buildings like children's blocks you can shift around at will. You see trains, airplanes, and occasionally a ship on the Main River. On clear days you can see out into the Taunus and Spessart regions. Guests never fail to exclaim in admiration, ''What a glorious place to work!'' Yet I never work up here. No matter how often I used to try, nothing ever came of it. The room did not fit into the pattern of our lives. Perhaps it was because no dog would negotiate the steep steps, or because I did not want to be constantly running downstairs if I had potatoes on the stove, or because in the early years here I had only one telephone; but when I had an extension installed upstairs, it was no improvement. While Urs was alive, our guests slept up here. It was always awkward; they had no running water, no bathroom, and if they wished to avoid going through our bedroom, they had to use the staircase out in the hall. Now and then we had a party up here, but that was inconvenient too, because everything had to be hauled up and down. In short, a handsome room that made everyone envious, but an utterly superfluous one.

My house in the Ticino is called "Mezzogiorno," because down below it the lake flows like a broad river toward the South, where I belong, where I feel at home. As fate will have it, I land in Holland, the northern flatlands; in the beginning I cry much of the time, preferring to live anywhere but there. No money for travel, no money for a car, but then we do take a trip, two days and two nights by train to Positano, which at the time is a village, with Moorish cubelike houses, a single hotel, and few bars. We walk along a ridge high above the sea, on a road traversed every few hours by a bus, now and then by a *carrozza*. We head west in the direction of Sorrento and east in the direction of Amalfi, along steep slopes covered with broom. Waiki and I, hand in hand, and I am so happy I wish I could die on the spot.

Cause of death: happiness—the sort of insane wish characteristic of the very young, possibly only so long as happiness is something concrete and objective, like typhus and pneumonia. That soon changes; now only unhappiness produces longing for death, a longing that becomes more and more abstract the closer one draws to the end, formless and distant, as feeble as one's pleasure in life.

* * *

I sit down in my yellow wing chair and light a cigarette, looking out toward the south. Not much of a view today; everything is gray and overcast. I can only hear the airplanes, not see them, but I have a sense of great expanses.

Curled up in the chair I doze a bit, suffused with well-being, relaxed. Suddenly this soothing lethargy is shattered by a question: Why did she not do away with Creon? That monster, insisting on law and order, his own version of law for the good of the state, his own system of order, which guaranteed smooth administration. Not law as Antigone conceived of it, a law that protected the interests of the individual; not the order she dreamed of, which helpfully regulated relations among people. It was easier for her to get to see him than for Stauffenberg to see Hitler; she was allowed to embrace him. How simple it is to assassinate a person as you embrace him.

Why did I not kill the SS captain during that great raid in June '43, when six thousand were hauled off at one time? I was wearing the armband of the Jewish Council, could move about freely, had only to go by him and pull the trigger. Of the revolver I did not have, but why not? Cyanide in my pocketbook, just in case—a selfish means of self-liberation. Why no revolver? Instead, wishing the Allies' planes would bomb us to bits.

What makes a person do a thing or not do it, the kind of thing that later on one cannot understand having done or not done? Why, instead of the unavailing discussion with Haverkamp, did I not try to have Waiki freed while he was still in Holland?

Why do I still say today: How terrible, frightful, intolerable? Why do I trot out this stereotyped response to most newspaper reports, radio broadcasts, television news programs? Why do I talk and do nothing?

Why do I have no notion of what I might do? As an individual you are helpless—Haverkamp's words of wisdom—nor do you want it otherwise; that would be pointless, too risky.

I am neither one of the rulers nor one of the oppressed. But what use do I make of my independence? Prey to creeping indifference, I go along with the silent majority, against my own better judgment.

Why do I allow the mass media to numb my imagination with an unending stream of superficial information? Why do I offer no resistance when Tuesday's earthquake fatalities are allowed to crowd out Monday's massacre victims? Plane crashes, bank holdups, hostage dramas, sex crimes, armed robberies produce a sort of temporary paralysis. Certain names stick in one's mind: My Lai, Lidice, Oradour. Why these in particular? Who has ever heard of Kalávrita, the town at the foot of the Chelmos, where according to legend one can find a spring whose waters cure rabies; I myself would never have heard of the town had we not taken the cog railway up there one evening, setting out the next morning to walk the twenty kilometers back to the sea. And I would not know the story of the place if that man from Patras had not been in our train compartment. He told us in broken English that the inhabitants of the town had supported the partisans; the Germans took revenge by shooting every man over the age of fifteen. The great white cross on the hillside—would we have thought to ask what it signified? How about the countless other crosses and the places without crosses, where instead of several hundred only one or two men were killed. Must one have seen it with one's own eyes before one can grasp it? And why does one always tend to consider the murder of many worse than the murder of a few?

Quantity as a multiplier of inhumanity. Why do we substitute sensationalism for sorrow?

And where has all the joy gone? The joy I used to feel. In two days Waiki is coming. Still forty-eight hours to go. If I spend three hours working on my report on Georg Büchner, it will be only forty-five. Then eight hours of sleep. When I get up: thirty-seven left. Tomorrow is almost here. Tomorrow Waiki will come. Or a hike in the mountains. A carnival ball. A trip. The latest Thomas Mann book, the latest Gide on my bedside table. Staying up all night reading.

There is no latest Thomas Mann book anymore, no latest Gide. And no equivalent. Or could I be mistaken? Perhaps I simply have not discovered it? More books than one can keep track of, and not one that I absolutely must have the day it comes out, that sweeps me with enthusiasm, entrances me, dashes my hopes, or makes me furious.

Living on memories. This stupid sense of superiority that cannot be shaken. Feeling so experienced. And simultaneously, uneasiness about the present. Fear of the future. The conviction that there will be nothing more. No love, no new friendships—is a new friendship really out of the question?—no change of scene, no more moves—except perhaps to an old-age home, that worst of all nightmares—my revulsion against other old people given permanence: Brueghel and Dante transported into our century amidst rubber plants, Dürer's rabbit, light bamboo furniture on yellow-flecked linoleum smelling of wax—fewer and fewer mountains, and eventually none at all, now and then an excursion, with steadily flagging spirit, my companions infuriated by my refrain: The first time I was here . . .

No, nothing more is in the offing. Deaths there

will be in plenty, and illnesses, my own and others', fatal ones and ones that pass but sap my energy. Weariness, inertia, longing for sleep that does not come. Drowsy days and sleepless nights, leaden indifference and ever fewer moments of clarity.

Why not do something about it? The pills are in the bathroom. Long ago I tried them out, and it was not painful. You fall rapidly into a deep sleep, gliding over into nothingness. Taking your life into your hands for the last time, before it is too late, before you stumble into humiliation, dimming consciousness, decay. Why not do it?

Perhaps a few people would cry for a while, though without despair. Not one of them would have lost anything of decisive value—the love of his life, the center of his universe. It is probable they would not even cry properly—they would just get watery eyes now and then, a twitching in the facial muscles, or a lump in the throat. My friends will comfort each other with the words that come so easily on such occasions: She was an intelligent woman, though not as intelligent as she liked to think, in the last years rather opinionated and crochety but, of course, that comes with age; on the whole a dear, much too nice to far too many people; whenever you wanted something of her, she was already taken up with others; she frittered away her life on that sort of thing, dissipated her talent. More and more these private obituaries veer off into criticism, coming to the inevitable conclusion: a good thing, actually, that it happened this way; how awful if she had dragged on, getting deafer and deafer and finally being totally isolated. I myself have voiced similar sentiments, always with a guilty conscience at the thought that I am doing the departed an injustice. When these sentiments are applied to me, they will no longer be able to hurt me, and I will no longer be able to laugh at them—more's the pity.

Why not do it? Right now, this very minute? Frau Multhaupt, the cleaning lady, does not come for another three days. That should be sufficient. She will find me, scream, and, much too excited to use the elevator, dash down the seven flights of stairs to find the building superintendent. Horrified and thrilled that such a thing should happen to her, her, who was like a mother to me—she is ten years younger, but that does not alter the fact that she treats me like a child, which is not only her fault but mine as well—Mevrouw Bartjes also treated me that way. She will tell the story over and over again: And then I found her on the bed, her mouth open and smeared with vomit. Oh, why did she do it, she was so well off. There— you see what ideas folks get when they have too much money. Then she will shake her head as she always does when something troubles her, and she will say, just like my intellectual friends: Who knows if it wasn't better this way. Just think what she was spared, with the world in such a crazy mess.

Why not do it? Right now, this very minute? Does my work hold me back? I am working on a book, am a writer, have published various things, though not that much; one might even call it very little for the number of years I have been at it. In the beginning there was Hitler—"the best years of our life"—interrupted university studies, photography instead of writing. Envied by many who had not learned any skill they could use as emigrés and were therefore forced to accept menial jobs.

Photography, a pleasant kind of work; after a little while in the darkroom you can already see what is going to develop. But do I want to see it? Filled with the urge to write, I instead find myself moving lamps around, raising and lowering them to illuminate tired exiles' faces or plunge round Dutch faces into an interesting chiaroscuro. I thrust toys into the hands of children and lie in wait for a little smile, which comes out beatific in the photograph. Children who are taken to be photographed must have beatific smiles; sobbing children are not in demand. They often do cry in the unfamiliar surroundings, with the harsh light. That is when I quickly shoot a few pictures for myself. I have an entire portfolio of weeping children.

Inexpressibly poignant wedding portraits in elegant or shabby hotels: Look this way, please, thank you, all done, let's try it once more. They all stare at my camera, the bride presses her bouquet against the white silk of her bosom . . .

For the most part it is Jews who ask me to do their wedding pictures. I meet a stratum of Jewish society I never encountered before: the petty bourgeoisie and proletariat, types Rembrandt painted, very Oriental, alien, suspicious toward outsiders, proud, tragic clowns, difficult to handle, and hard to take for me, who am not one of them, who am one of them, an assimilated Jew without religious ties who shares their fate, a fate that extends back thousands of years and forward into the immediate future. After the portrait, a piece of wedding cake: "There you are, young lady, for you, enjoy." I try to smile arrogantly, which comes across as shyness, do not say "Crap!" or say it so quietly that no one hears me, and eat my cake, which is far too sweet. The element of amusement outweighs the humiliation.

Yet such moments are rare; it is not amusing in the slightest when a *mevrouw*—she, too, Jewish—who was supposed to come by to pick up her photographs, calls up to say she must ask me to deliver them after all, and this at six-thirty, when I have a rendezvous with Waiki at the movies. When I refuse, she shouts into the telephone, "That's what one gets for taking one's business to foreigners." Lashing out at the minority, and I dare not say a word in my own defense. I am merely tolerated here, and my residence permit, for which I had to wait in line for hours at the aliens' registration bureau, is valid for only a year.

In hiding I paint ceramic animals for Kurt and his wife, who sell them to department stores. For a year, and then that too comes to an end, when we can no longer obtain clay or paint: hundreds of tigers, elephants, seals. A prisoner's work in a prison to which I consigned myself. Sometimes I think: If only I had gone along on that fatal adventure. The sort of thing one thinks.

Twelve years during which I do not write a line, the most decisive period in a person's life, when there is the best inspiration, the most energy.

After the war I finally manage to write a couple of books. They deal with war and deportation. I have nothing else to write about. The key to my life.

And now Antigone. The day will come when this book too will be finished. The day when I commend it to its grave like a beloved being. Nothing will remain. In the middle of the night I wake with a start: I want to be dead. Longing for death, always lurking in the background, becomes clamorous.

Waiki brushes his hand over my forehead: "You're anticipating it." I do not ask what I am anticipating, because I know, as I always do when he says something elliptical. It is death, but Waiki is thinking of his own, whereas I am thinking of ours. I see us as one person and am convinced that neither of us will survive the other for so much as a moment.

He has been dead for two weeks—if the Gestapo has given the correct date, which I do not doubt, in view of the bureaucratic pedantry with which the murder machine operates—by the time I learn of it. Waiki is dead, and I am still alive. We are not one person but two.

I wish for death, which does not come; a broken heart is a poetic metaphor without medical validity. Yet, as a feeling of emptiness begins to replace the pain, even this wish vanishes into thin air.

Emptiness is empty, there is nothing left—no happiness, no unhappiness. Emptiness is hollow—I am being hollowed out, becoming a hollow fraud. I do whatever seems appropriate at the moment: sleep, get dressed, work, talk, even laugh. I behave normally so the others will not notice I am a robot someone has wound up. Robots do not die, they break down. I do not break down, a tough cookie, as they say; I let myself be swept along by the current, swept back to Germany.

I walk through the ruins and feel they belong there; when a world has been destroyed, no buildings should remain unscathed. I travel in overcrowded trains with cackling hens and smelly rabbits. I buy butter on the black market but do not have enough money for cigarettes. In Munich I eat my first ice cream after the war; it has a taste and texture like sand. I go to the premiere of a ballet at the Prinzregenten Theater, carrying a bundle of wriggling whitefish I have just managed to obtain. I dare not leave them in the cloakroom because anything edible is stolen, so I take them to my seat. I move in with Urs, my friend from earlier times. For years I carry two passports, a German one and a stateless person's one, which I later exchange for a Dutch passport, and I am so well trained from my period of living underground that I always present the right one.

Gradually everything gets better, or worse, as the

case may be; it depends on your point of view. No longer is Urs obliged to dress his singers in threadbare robes from the costume room; the stage designers conjure up splendid costumes, and the visual effects overpower the human content. And such wonderful effects they are—at first one resists, then one gives in, fuming and fussing but still going along with it. Remember the *Threepenny Opera:* ''The bulging pocket makes the easy life''—and who would not want that?

The few years I have left—that's what one says from fifty on, when one begins to worry about whether one's pension will provide enough to live on. One says it so often that it becomes automatic. Who knows, perhaps I will live to be one hundred; more and more people are living that long, not that I would ever want to be that old, not even eighty, or eighty at most.

I repress the thought of death as death draws nearer. The sense of immortality is gone, and I behave exactly like the society around me, which makes a shameful secret of dying, hiding it in hospitals. Even the death of Urs, the person closest to me, is masked by the hospital rituals and the problems connected with reorganizing my own life. Only in the case of my dog, the creature I should have protected but failed to protect, does death catch me unawares. I am distraught almost to the point of madness. I brush along walls, getting gray paint on my clothes, cobwebs in my hair, yet I lack the strength to ram through the wall, to go really mad, to let myself fall into unknown spaces, unfathomed depths.

What makes Antigone so fascinating: that she, so close to death, should love life. That she has the courage to gamble away life. Her unsurpassed courage, which accepts any and every challenge. Without a moment's hesitation she does what she considers imperative. Leaves Thebes with Oedipus, while Polyneices, whom she loves, stays behind. The blind man needs her. She decides quickly, does what she thinks is right. She understands the art of living and the art of dying as two aspects of a great unity. In light of all she experienced, I cannot imagine her ever returning to a comfortable royal-bourgeois existence. An existence in which everything runs smoothly, in which her every desire is met. She does not want fulfillment; she wants her dream.

I go downstairs to the bathroom and open the medicine cabinet. There are the pills. A hundred of them in a brown bottle with a screw lid. Next to them twenty suppositories in a little box. This time pumping out my stomach will not help. Will not hurt. I unscrew the lid, take out the wad of cotton, shake a few pills into my hand. I slide them from one hand to the other. This is how princesses play with pearls.

Back and forth, from one hand to the other. For a long time. Then I pour them back into the bottle, squeeze in the cotton, screw on the top, and put them back, next to the suppositories. My palms are covered with white powder. I lick it off. It tastes bitter. I gargle with mouthwash, apply lipstick, and leave the bathroom.

8

In the living room I sit down at my desk, open the notebook from which I ripped out the pages, and begin to revise them. It goes quickly and easily; I enjoy revising, and my translations have given me a certain facility at it, which I lack when doing first drafts. And a good thing, too; I would not want to be the kind of writer who writes according to formula.

I work for more than an hour, smoking without pause, then begin to lose the train of thought; my concentration wavers. I suddenly remember that I must make out a check to pay for the last tune-up of my BMW—I have been carrying the bill around in my pocketbook for a week. Actually, one is supposed to pay cash for service. There is a large sign to that effect posted in the service department, but apparently I inspire enough confidence for them to let me take the car without having paid. Inspiring confidence in others makes a number of things easier. I shamelessly smuggle cigarettes into Germany from Switzerland, not only because they are cheaper there but also because I get a kick out of it. Not once have I had to open my car trunk; a gray-haired old lady with a strikingly handsome dog is apparently above suspicion. Perhaps that will change now; perhaps an old lady traveling alone without a dog is particularly suspect.

Habits formed long ago. There was a time when

the penalty for smuggling was death. If caught, you went off with the next transport. That meant being shipped to the gas chambers at Auschwitz. In spite of that I smuggled countless letters out of the Joodsche Schouwburg—the collecting point for those of Amsterdam's Jews slated for deportation—putting the letters in my brassiere, in the lining of my coat, which had a special zipper for the purpose, or, when I was in a hurry, simply in my handbag: letters to people the prisoners hoped, usually in vain, to receive help from.

Then there were the officially sanctioned letters that I was supposed to type and for whose content I was responsible. Jews who had been pulled out of their beds in the middle of the night stood in line to reach my desk, where they dictated instructions to friends and relatives, telling them to bring things they had forgotten when they had to leave in such a hurry, often vitally important things like winter coats and sturdy shoes—presumably vitally important, for one can hardly say something is vitally important when people are embarking on a journey toward death. They also asked for unbelievably superfluous things, like decks of cards, writing paper, coffee cups, sofa cushions. Never books. Where was the people of scribes and Talmudic scholars now? Waiki had once said, "When God took everything from the Jews, at least he left them the gift of reading." Now that too was gone. No one requested that particular source of comfort. Nothing could comfort them. (In the many months I worked in the Schouwburg, one lone young man complained he had been forced to leave behind the second volume of *Crime and Punishment*, which he had been reading. I was planning to bring him my own copy the next evening, but by that time he had already been taken away.)

The shock, the sense of utter helplessness, reduced them all to the same level. The letters dictated to me were all alike, whether their authors were professors or workers, East European Jews, German Jews, or Dutch Jews. I kept an eye out for a veiled or open declaration of love for the recipient, a cry of outrage or an expression of resignation. Nothing of the sort came. And another thing disturbed me profoundly. None of them cried. It would have been so natural, so liberating, but no tears came. Submissive, already no longer of this world, the *morituri* filed past.

I typed and typed, far into the night, sometimes all night long: I, a regularly employed though unpaid member of the Jewish Council, Expositure Division. No one knew what the word *expositure* was supposed to signify. The dictionary of foreign terms gave the meanings "external branch of a business" and "branch church." A branch church of the Gestapo? Was this some SS man's macabre joke? We had one thing in common with the Gestapo: our assignments protected us—them from service on the front, us from deportation. But only for a while. Only until Amsterdam was purged of Jews. Hence, it served the interests of both groups to maintain the status quo as long as possible.

One Sunday in July 1942—no one has heard anything definite about deportations, and we simply ignore the rumors about the operation getting under way this afternoon—the Dutch police deliver a notice printed on cheap green paper to my building. It informs me that I should get ready for assignment to "a work detail under police supervision in Germany." I will be allowed to take along this item and that, must register at such and such a place, my train will depart at such and such a time from Central Station, bound for the Dutch transit camp at Westerbork.

Up to now no one over forty has received such a notice, and there is no reason to suspect that "work" is merely a euphemism. Not until weeks later will children, the aged, the mentally ill, the sick and dying be summoned to deportation on exactly the same pretext.

No clear knowledge, but a glimmering of how slight the chances are of surviving. Finally fate is coming to my aid, turning over to others the suicide I failed to carry out after Waiki's death because I did not wish to subject my mother to the same thing that had just been done to me. Going into hiding is out of the question. The Germans have already threatened to send one Jew to Mauthausen for every Jew who goes into hiding. Mauthausen: for all of us that name has become synonymous with nameless terror. Infinitely worse than "work detail." The Gestapo knows that and skillfully and brutally exploits our fear. The threat proves so effective that it is never carried out. Only later does it become clear that no one is being sent to that dread place in someone else's stead. After that, nothing prevents people from going into hiding. But when the deportations begin, there is only one hope of salvation: the Jewish Council.

My Antigone notebook tumbles to the floor as I hastily stand up. I rush to the window, throw it open, and take a deep breath, drawing the awful air, laden with soot and gasoline fumes, down into my lungs, then shut the window, light a cigarette, and pace about the room. I notice things I have long since ceased to notice: the beautiful simplicity of the Frankfurt wardrobe chest, the cigarette burn in the sofa upholstery, the three-legged Danish chairs, which make a sort of ideological statement in and of themselves. I dislike ideologies, I dislike the chairs. I look at the original Picasso print, a portrait of Dora

Maar, signed by the artist. What does this woman mean to me? Why has she been staring past me all these years, her one eye looking out from the picture, the other seen in profile? This arrogant, spiteful stranger whom I never had the slightest desire to meet. I bought the print in the intoxication of the postwar period, when it seemed so wonderful to be in touch with the international art scene once more. Urs always liked it better than I, and it was simply out of inertia and habit that I left it on my wall after he died. What perverse demands pictures make on us: they want to hang there forever. I would not want to hear the same piece of music or read the same book over and over again.

Ash from my cigarette drops onto the rug. I spread it around with my foot, rubbing it in until there is no more to be seen, then go back to my desk, pick up the notebook, and sit down.

I try to write, without success, then mull over all the improvements I should make in the apartment, even though I know I will undertake none of them. Suddenly the Jewish Council is there again.

The morning after I receive the summons I go for a walk with my friend Alice, an "Aryan" German, in the windswept fields south of the city. "You must get into the Jewish Council," she says, "it's your duty. Dear girl, haven't you ever had to do your duty? You can't simply skip out on your mother, that would be pure selfishness, it would stink to high heaven. You mustn't do that. Don't be so hardhearted, don't be so stubborn. There is no other alternative. You know how much your mother loved Waiki. Do you want to take her other child away from her, too? You have no right to kill her. You must get into the Jewish Council."

I shake my head, say "No."

"But that's the only way you can protect her." I continue to say no, but with less and less conviction. "You have only one obligation," Alice says, "and that is to get your mother through the war. After that you can do whatever you please."

Suicides, once postponed, never get carried out. She knows that as well as I do. She wants to save not only my mother but me as well. "You must," she says, "you must." She repeats the same thing for two hours. Then I give in. Give in as usual to that "you must, you must." Beaten down, exhausted, capable of only one thought: for my mother's sake—I must protect my mother, must not abandon her. I start to cry. Before it is all over, Alice cries too. Tears in our eyes, we hurry along. The wind takes our breath away, and we pant, running from ourselves, from this doomed city, whose lovely, delicate skyline is visible on our left. O Alice, O Amsterdam.

Members of the Jewish Council are not required to leave. They are performing their work detail in Holland, the Germans explain cynically. Helping the Germans deport other Jews. Helping them, and by so doing gaining an opportunity to slow the pace of the deportations. Going through the motions of helping while actually committing sabotage. The Jewish Council has many sides to it. On the one hand there are the two presiding officers, who do whatever they are told, "to prevent even worse things from occurring." And on the other hand there is Walter Süskind, who risks his life to smuggle thousands of children, hundreds of adults out of the Schouwburg.

A criminal organization, a naive organization, used as camouflage by a few courageous souls? I am not criminally inclined, not naive, not a hero.

Curiously enough, neither Alice nor I doubt for a moment that I will be accepted into the Jewish Council if I want to be. It is a question of knowing people, having connections. "Vitamin C" is the term used in the grisly jargon of the times. And in fact the Jewish Council is a class-oriented organization, and that is yet another aspect of it. An organization run by professors, lawyers, and successful businessmen, who give preferential protection to their own kind. Of course, they also accept proletarians from the Jewish quarter—for a time, half the Jews in Amsterdam are members—because the huge organization needs porters, chauffeurs, messengers, cooks, and seamstresses.

When I begin to call my connections into play that afternoon, I discover that I do not need special patronage in order to be admitted. Waiki's death is my patronage. The steering committee has determined that anyone who has lost a close relative in Mauthausen will be hired automatically. (The euphemism "lost" is still used. Even in the throes of death they would rather cling to the conventions than face the truth that it was murder.)

My first assignment is at once terrible and ludicrous. Terrible for me, ludicrous in itself. The Germans have a rule—enforced only during the first few weeks, then never mentioned again—that all those about to be transported must be photographed, with numbers pinned to their chests. Mug shots. We do not know what the pictures are used for, in whose hands they will end up.

The first phase of the deportation, when the Germans tried to get young Jews to report for work details, has proved a failure. Only very few were so foolish as to turn themselves in. Now the poorest of the poor, who have no connections and cannot defend themselves, are being dragged out of their dwellings in the Jewish quarter. I snap their pictures:

no more beatifically smiling children for their parents, no crying children for myself, just children with huge, grave eyes full of age-old sorrow, adults with my own eyes, except that mine are grayish blue, not brown and shadowed. Why is my iris different? Does environment affect pigmentation? I am ashamed of my eyes, of my freedom, of my good clothes, I am ashamed of my Leica, and yet I go on snapping the shutter. I have been assigned to this task, no one is harmed by it but me, and so I do it. That is how people behave, and I am no exception.

Antigone does not behave this way. Obstinate, absolutely certain that she is right. Yet is she really right? Everything ambiguous, at once reasonable and excessive. Right and wrong tragically obscure. There is talk of her flowerlike nature, then of the woman of action who is passionately one-sided, then of the most sisterly of souls, the bacchante of death, the heroic exemplification of resistance. What would she have done in my position? Would she have preserved her integrity? Acted to protect her mother? The two were irreconcilable. I think of her with envy, for all she had to do was bury the dead, not try to save the living. She was alone. Being alone—an incomparable source of strength.

After my photographing, the Schouwburg. A shabby old theater, stale air, the reek of sweat, disinfectant. The stage and the auditorium emptied out except for the seats in the balcony. The lobby filled with mattresses on which prisoners sleep. Jewish prisoners, destined for deportation—that much they know —for extermination—that they do not know. The passion play of the twentieth century. Endgame. The Amsterdam Schouwburg. The soccer stadium of Santiago. There is no torture in the Schouwburg. Sometimes they beat someone up, now and then one hears slaps, once a woman shouts, "You ought to be ashamed of yourself!" to an SS corporal who in a rage is shaking the contents of prisoners' bundles onto the floor. She is made to stand on a chair for hours. But the interrogations, the tortures take place elsewhere, at Gestapo headquarters, in the prisons.

The proceedings are not cruel, hardly even loud. Once set in motion, the machinery functions smoothly, grinds on and on, preparing fuel for the ovens in Poland. Not cruel, unless you happen to see the cold perfection of the whole thing as the most extreme form of cruelty. Yet those who enter here have not abandoned all hope. They cling to hope for all they are worth.

There even exists the possibility that some of the prisoners will get out and use the short period before being rearrested to go into hiding. One may have the right sort of stamp on his papers, another may be a diamond cutter and as such essential for the armaments industry, yet another may be interceded for by some influential person. Then he is set free by the Germans, legally. Others, especially children, are set free illegally by us. At night, when no more prisoners are being brought in, we members of the Jewish Council huddle together in Süskind's room and discuss those we might smuggle out. Each of us has personal preferences: family members, friends, acquaintances, protégés among the prisoners we have just met. The talk goes back and forth: Yes, we could get that one out, no, impossible, too old, unreliable, too well known, has already attracted too much attention, too clumsy, he'll be right back here in three days, that would make no sense. Süskind, small and stocky, with close-cropped blond hair and large blue eyes, wily like Odysseus, combat-ready like Achilles, Süskind, the hero, the savior, the gambler, says yes, says no, selects, decides on life or death. He assumes the responsibility, gets the Germans drunk, falsifies lists, knows all the tricks, invents new ones, knows which nights are safe, always gets away with it, and yet himself perishes in the end at Auschwitz, along with his wife and child.

Our work in the Schouwburg is done in shifts, day and night. I am always on at night, by choice, for I do not mind it, and if my mother is brought in, I want to be there. The likelihood of getting her out is good if I am around.

Every evening I make the long trip by bicycle from my apartment to the Schouwburg. On the Fiets, the main shopping street, there is a blue blackout lantern, which gives hardly any light. The first time, I cry from tension and fear of the dark stinking water in the canal. Then I become accustomed to it.

The old and the sick are picked up by day as well. One time they bring in Waiki's eighty-year-old grandmother. I ask Süskind to assign me to the train detail so that I can make the last half hour easier for her. I sit beside her on the wooden seat. Not until they reach Westerbork will she be shoved into a cattle car and shipped off to Poland. I stroke her hand while a man in the compartment talks at me incessantly: "My son is in Mauthausen. Of course, they notified me of his death. But I just don't believe he is dead. Not for a moment. It's impossible that so many young people would just up and die that way. These death notices are pure sadism on the part of the Gestapo." I do not contradict him. I have witnessed this type of naive denial all too often. I nod, seemingly in agreement, but close to tears.

I must not cry now, must not make the parting even harder on the old lady. "Do you think I'll be back?"

"Of course you'll be back. The war won't go on much longer." I hesitate before I add, "And then Waiki will come back, too."

Outside they have just shouted, "All members of the Jewish Council out!" I fail to react in time, and hear the doors being locked. I rattle at the door to my car without success. A young baggage handler realizes my plight and calls to me, "Wait, I'll get a key." The SS captain on the platform hears him and orders, "No key is to be fetched. Anyone who fails to pay attention goes along." The boy positions himself under the window and spreads his arms: "Jump!" I kiss the old woman once more, open the window, and leap. The SS captain looks on in silent amusement.

I must not let myself think about the Jewish Council anymore. Yet the harder I try to banish these thoughts, the more they obsess me, and I plunge deeper and deeper into these buried memories. Into the leaden stillness created by an inability to weep. And suddenly there it is, the Event, the ultimate humiliation.

A smell of creosote, blended with the odor of cigarettes and leather, that accompanies the man recently installed as the SS commander of the Schouwburg because the Gestapo found his predecessor too lax. We members of the Jewish Council stand around, fifty or sixty of us, while he stammers and raves at us, delivering what he considers a speech. As he nears the end, he suddenly becomes lucid, saying in a sinister soft voice: "You are here to guard the prisoners, and I categorically forbid you to speak with the prisoners any more than necessary. Is that clear? Anyone who disobeys will be shipped out with the prisoners."

No one stirs, no one speaks. I want to step forward and say: I am not a prison guard. I am the same as those I am supposed to guard, a Jew, a human being.

I want to, but I do not. My mind is racing. What would happen if I did? Perhaps he would strike me in the face—that would be liberating, it would give my hatred a channel into which it could flow, on and on, without beginning or end, life again at last, carrying me swiftly and surely toward love, toward death, for I would be shipped out with the others. But then there is my mother and the responsibility I have assumed for protecting her. I know their modus operandi: she would be seized immediately, for the Germans say, "We do not wish to separate families"; in reality it is their policy to make an entire family pay for the transgressions of one of its members. I cannot deliver her into their clutches, must not give voice to my hatred.

Time passes. The SS man has dismissed us, and all the others are crowding around me, moving toward the exit, carrying me along with them. I submit, silent like the others.

Sitting here bent over my Antigone notebook, I become aware of the filth I have waded through, the icy coldness when I found myself confronted with decisions that could not but make me guilty, no matter how I chose.

9

I can no longer bear being alone in the apartment. I pull my coat off the hanger and dash out. The elevator takes its time. I shift my weight impatiently from one foot to the other. Finally it arrives and starts on its way down, stopping unexpectedly on the third floor, where my retired elderly neighbor gets on (he is probably younger than I), the one who keeps inviting me out to Sachsenhausen to try the apple wine and never takes offense at the pretexts I find for refusing. He tips his hat and asks, "Is something wrong with your dog?—I always see you alone these days."

"He's dead."

"But he wasn't that old. Did you have him put to sleep?" I nod. "Was he sick?"

"No, he wasn't sick." Let him go ahead and think I had a perfectly healthy dog put to sleep, let him consider me a murderer if that will make him leave me in peace.

"I s'pose he was becoming a nuisance. You're too old for such a big dog, anyway. A dachshund would be better. I can give you the address of a good kennel. My sister has a friend—"

"No, thank you, no dachshund." In the meantime we have left the building. To shake him off, I go into the nearest store, a drugstore, and buy a bottle of eau de cologne that I neither need nor use.

I cross the park, heading toward the city. Where else to go on a gray November day? Where do old ladies go? To a café, the zoo, the palm garden, a movie? To the doctor's, where they can kill time in the waiting room and then are given five or ten minutes to explain what is wrong with them? And what is wrong with them? Everything and nothing; they have the most terrible, the ultimate incurable illness: old age.

Yesterday on television the soldiers' widows whose pensions were reduced on their husbands' sixty-fifth birthdays because at that age the men would have retired. They all said, "He'll be sixty-five in December," or "He turned sixty-five in July." Probably the bureaucrats who dreamed up this grotesque system of reductions find it perfectly normal that the women should speak this way, so many years later, as if nothing had happened. They sat there tired and mousy in their kitchens or living rooms, excited and flustered because they were on television and were supposed to demonstrate, with all eyes upon them and their marriage portraits on the wall, how faithful they had been and how miserably faithfulness is rewarded. Had they really been so faithful?

I walk along tiresome, faceless streets laid out through what was once one of the most beautiful historic old cities. I have walked through so many cities that I sometimes think my whole life has consisted of nothing else. Driven by my fascination with beauty and ugliness, with people, by the wish to remain anonymous, not to have to speak and yet be surrounded by human beings speaking with one another, to see things not intended for my eyes, to observe joy and pain without feeling them; to receive impressions, to watch and take note, perhaps to exchange a few words with someone, in a foreign tongue, noncommittally, merely in order to feel myself.

Walking through cities—Amsterdam, Munich, Paris, at once familiar and alien, threatening, the air leaden, walls, nothing but walls, early morning or late evening, deep silence, much deeper than it can ever really be in a city; then echoing footsteps, soldiers in high boots wheel around a corner; they wear green uniforms, sometimes gray, visored caps or battle helmets, not necessarily German ones, also English, American, or of unknown origin. They have their guns at the ready, or no guns at all. They march toward me, very slowly or very rapidly, block my path and demand—and this always in German—to see my papers. Usually I have none, which simplifies matters; sometimes I have forged ones, which I offer to them. They examine the documents, shining a flashlight through them, sniffing them or licking them. They recognize the forgery, grin, take me with them, pushing me along toward the black wall.

Walls, nothing but walls. A light blue silken sky full of clouds over Amsterdam, salty air, the proximity of the ocean, which I may not go near; people who wear the yellow star with the word *Jood* printed on it are not allowed to leave the city. I haul my cameras, tripods, and lamps around, forbidden to use the trolley or a taxi. In my sandals I stumble against a stone and break my little toe; the pain is intense, so much so that I expect to faint, but I do not keel over; I stand there until I no longer see bright spots before my eyes. I wipe away my tears and collect my things; I cannot simply abandon these most precious possessions, with which I earn my living. A few months later the Germans take them from me, and I learn how to improvise to keep from starving.

People I do not know greet me, saluting the yellow

star. The Dutch declare their solidarity, are willing to risk their lives for us, let us hide out in their houses, store our possessions for us—my books survive the war in the house of Mimi, the resistance fighter, who in 1945 is liberated from the Ravensbrück concentration camp just in the nick of time, for she is gravely ill. They furnish us with forged identity papers, with food, they pass off Jewish children as their own, but they cannot prevent our being deported. They stand by and watch when the Germans come to get us, and can do nothing else, for what good is an unarmed population against armed occupation troops? Resistance flares up, is crushed, sometimes achieves small successes with deeds done in obscurity and reported by the grapevine. We hear about some, but there are many things we never hear about; much gets lost in the interminable boredom of waiting for something we do not want to happen. The boredom of sitting by a deathbed, the voice growing ever fainter, the breathing shallower, the patient more distant. Why don't you just die and get it over with! One day like the next, the news always the same: the Germans victorious, X deported, Y arrested, Z a suicide.

I am in my mid-thirties, longing for a man, and find Joschi, a married man, a Hungarian Jew, a psychotherapist, melancholy, submissive to God's will, intelligent, and in his better moments capable of subtle humor. We see each other every Sunday morning; I do not know why it cannot be at any other time and have no idea what he tells his wife—nor do I care. We are very distant with one another, always using the formal mode of address. Our program never varies: intercourse, then playing chess, to avoid having to discuss the terrible situation all the time. "Check," he says, and something like triumph flashes in his sorrowful eyes as for a few minutes he, the victim, is a victor.

Walls, walls without end. Boulders heaped upon boulders, Cyclops-fashion. Walls that render life easier for the city, or more difficult. Keeping enemies at bay. Separating people from others.

One brother inside, the other outside the walls. Poised for battle. As if there were no better means than the sword, as if human language did not exist for settling disputes. But on either side words have failed. There is no desire to negotiate. Both want to perish.

Her heart beats for the one who has come as an enemy, who is laying siege to the city. It was his wish she should return to Thebes. Hard to say whether it was a request or an order—he gives orders gently and makes requests imperiously. It is not clear whether he would have accepted a refusal.

Keep still, wait, circulate. Observe everything, speak with as many people as possible. Prepare the ground for him, seek out those who are willing to go over to his side and topple Creon once the fighting begins.

Some respond to the barest of hints, hold out their hands and whisper: Amazing how much you resemble him. If you were not dressed in girl's clothing, you might be mistaken for him. It is good you are here at least, in his place.

But too few smile, and they are the wrong ones: small tradesmen, girls at the fountain, now and then a soldier when no officer is in sight. People who can accomplish nothing, the powerless.

Here is the pharmacy where I bought that medicinal paste the day before yesterday. I warm it up and apply it to my ankles to make them feel better. A Swiss product ordered just for me. The woman pharmacist mentioned pointedly when I came in that she had another package of it, but I insisted I wanted only one. In the meantime I have changed my mind, go inside, am handed the package, and am taken aback when the woman says, "That will be fifteen marks."

"Last time it cost only twelve-fifty."

The woman raises her eyebrows and says, in the tone incompetent teachers reserve for five-year-olds, "You must be mistaken."

"I'm absolutely certain."

"No, madam, you just don't remember. That often happens to people at your age."

I give her the fifteen marks. As I am leaving the shop I reach into my coat pocket and pull out the old receipt. Glance at it. Twelve-fifty. I do not go back in, do not say: You discriminated against me because of my age. I swallow the insult, begin to walk very rapidly, then slow down, passing the old Jewish cemetery with its high walls and the gate that is usually kept locked. For a moment I feel a surge of sentimental solidarity with those lying inside. I identify with their insecurity and timorousness, their watchful intelligence.

In the display of a ladies' clothing shop on Berlinerstrasse there is a rust brown sweater I like. For the past few days I have stopped and looked at it every time I went by. It is not particularly expensive, but not cheap, either; solidly in the middle, like the whole store. Should I? Shouldn't I? Do I need it? Nonsense—I have heaps of sweaters at home. Yet it would be nice to own it. But perhaps it is too big for me, or too small, or it is not so becoming to me as I imagine. Hesitation, indecision. When I was younger I would have gone right in the first time I saw it and tried it on. Just trying things on was such fun that it was worth the effort.

Shortly before I received notification of Waiki's death, when he was already dead but I did not yet know, I bought myself a dress. I was not eating or sleeping properly, had lost weight, looked like a ghost, was dying one painful death after another. And yet at a certain moment I went into a chic little store and purchased the most elegant dress I had ever owned. The last spark of hope, not really a spark, just a faint glow that I tried to fan into flames. For the half hour I was in the shop, and perhaps only a few minutes of that time, I played the role of the young woman adorning herself for her absent beloved. For the last time. That I knew.

One more glance at the sweater. Perhaps tomorrow, I think, and continue my walk. Only as far as the next window, which is filled with antique jewelry. In its midst a *Biedermeier* chain, like one I used to have. Thin, hammered gold decorated with delicate blue and white enamelwork. I had earrings and a brooch to match, the set my great-grandmother wears in the beautiful portrait that now hangs in my house in the Ticino. This jewelry almost cost me my life.

When the deportations begin, those Jews who happen to be in prison are shipped off immediately. Not long before that, a tall, lean Dutchman in civilian dress appears at my apartment. "I am from the Doelenstraat office. I presume you know what that is." I do know: the headquarters of the Dutch SS. "Do you know a Mevrouw Bartjes?"

"Yes."

"She works for you."

"No, she used to be my cleaning lady. Since Jews have been forbidden to employ Christians in their homes, she has stopped working here, of course." A lie. But prearranged with Mevrouw Bartjes. I add, "But she still visits me occasionally."

"Why?"

"Because we are friends."

"I see. So you are friends with your cleaning lady. And although you know it is forbidden, you also gave her your jewelry for safekeeping." I deny it vehemently. I think of the three crammed suitcases Frau Bartjes is storing for me. With bed linens embroidered with my initials. "I must search your apartment."

"As you like." I follow him around, trying to imagine what he expects to find, since he must be searching for objects that are not here. In the kitchen I have a bowl filled with eggs. Eggs can no longer be obtained legally.

"Where did you get these?"

"On the black market." My boldness pays off. His tone becomes friendlier, and he says before leaving that I should stop by the Doelenstraat office toward evening.

Should I go? Should I not go? Not going would mean going into hiding at once, going would mean prison. I have nowhere to hide. No forged papers. Nothing is ready. So I decide to go.

He is alone in the dimly lit office on Doelenstraat. My jewelry is lying on his desk. "You lied to me." Mevrouw Bartjes must have handed over the jewelry, but not the suitcases. I sigh with relief and say, "This jewelry no longer belongs to me."

"You gave it to her for safekeeping."

"That's true. But I also told her that if anything should happen to me, it was hers. They murdered my husband in Mauthausen, that's what happened to me. The jewelry belongs to Mevrouw Bartjes." I speak the word *murdered* in a loud, firm voice. Look directly at him as I say it. He lowers his eyes. Brushes his hand across his forehead. Not a sound is to be heard.

Suddenly he says, "I shall report that I did not find anything. Will you be alone in your apartment in the morning the day after tomorrow."

"Yes."

"I shall come then and return your jewelry."

He comes, and I am alone. I expect he will want to sleep with me. But he merely bows stiffly and hands over my jewelry. "Do you have children?" I ask, perplexed.

"A boy and a girl."

"Bring them to me. I'd like to photograph them for you—to express my gratitude."

"Very kind of you. I'll do that." And with that he leaves. That same day I take the jewelry to Mevrouw Bartjes and give it to her for keeps. The children never do turn up.

Another display window. It belongs to a hunting goods store, which does not interest me. Nevertheless I stop there to look, trying to prolong my walk into town, to give it content. Among the rifles, loden jackets, and field glasses, a copy of the magazine *Hound and Quarry*. Five years ago I bought myself an issue and circled the advertisements that offered Münsterland pups, then got into my car and drove from kennel to kennel until I had found the handsomest mother with the most lively pups. I feel strongly tempted now. But I do not want another dog, and certainly not another hunting dog. I am wretched at raising dogs, inconsistent in my obedience-training, obsessed with the desire to give the animal a good life. To leave him perfectly free. A ridiculous undertaking in a city apartment on the eighth floor. And yet . . . With a few brief interruptions I have always had a dog. Life without a dog is hollow—no walks, no creature to talk to, to stroke, no warm animal body on my bed. I am not allowed to have another dog. Too old. Too old, that's what my mind says, but not my heart—this wrenching conflict. In everything I do. Everything I want to do, yet leave undone. No *Hound and Quarry* this time. Move on.

I enter a crafts shop, simply in order to talk with someone and handle various objects. The talking part is soon attended to. "May I help you?" the saleswoman asks.

"No, thank you, I'd just like to look around." I go from shelf to shelf, now and then touching something, picking up a glass piece, running my hand over a woven mat. Most of the things are pleasing, tasteful, superfluous.

On a table already handsomely decorated for Christmas, I find a number of toys. I reach for a cylindrical object covered in patterned paper and hold it up to my eye. It is a very simply made kaleidoscope. Every time I turn it, the fragments of glass tumble into a different position, forming a new six-pointed star of incomparable beauty. I turn and turn, cannot get my fill, am relaxed and blissful. In a magnificent microcosm like this there are no concentration camps and no murders, no pain and no old age. The Romantics' ideal realm of beautiful appearances. And "in the end, everything, everything is good."

I must have this magical object, clutch it as if I were afraid someone might snatch it from me, reluctantly surrender it for wrapping, pay, press the package to my chest, the secret treasure I need only turn before my eye if I wish to leave reality behind. A fleeting, treacherous dream, a bold, lovely illusion that one can see the invisible, create wholeness out of nothing. Then the happiness is destroyed by a sudden stab of pain—no, not pain, anger at the thought of death so near, with no possibility of escape. The trap has snapped shut.

Up into the tower at the Dirke Gate. She asks the guards to move a bit to one side so that she can gaze down for a moment, only a moment, on the seven enemy armies. "We cannot let you do that, Princess, it is too dangerous. Even we are not allowed to stand here without helmets and shields."

"Then give me a helmet and shield for a moment."

The man hesitates, shakes his head, then decides to yield, takes off his helmet and shield, and hands them to her. "But just for a moment, Princess."

Wearing the helmet, which is too big for her, and carrying the heavy, leather-covered wooden shield, she goes to the very edge of the rampart. The sun dazzles her. She holds up her hand to block it out, at the same time pushing back the helmet. Squints into the greenish yellowish glare, the soft gray haze of dust, looking around, trying to orient herself: over there is the winding blue Ismen River, over there the Dirke spring. To the right the grave of Zethus and Amphion, to the left the grave of Niobe's seven daughters. In between, a confused tumult of men, horses, and chariots. The sentry has come forward without his helmet and shield, keeping up a steady stream of talk: "The big man with the white plume on his helmet is Count Hippomedon; that one with the long shield who looks more like a barbarian than a Greek is Tydeus, brother-in-law to Prince Polyneices. The one who is leading his horses over there, probably to sacrifice them, is the seer Amphiaraus, and that one who is measuring the ramparts must be Capaneus." She lets him talk on while her eyes range over the crowd, searching for one and only one. Where is he? Now a suit of golden armor catches the light near the grave of Niobe's daughters. A golden helmet, the man takes a few steps, yes, that is his gait, that must be he. So far, so near, beloved and inaccessible, Polyneices, Polyneices. Oh, to be able to fly to him, to fling her arms around him, to sweep him away from the imprisoning circle of the armies to the grove, the olive grove outside the South Gate, their refuge as children, where the sun played on the narrow silvery leaves and brought a glow to the moss, dotted with wild cyclamen. To feel his hand on her hair once again, to see his mocking mouth and his gentle eyes, to hear his deep voice and his dry laugh. And he will take off the golden armor, stretch out in the moss, and lure her: Come, Antigone, my one and only sisterly bride, let us lie together and conceive a son with raven-black hair and starry eyes, who will lead our people out of bondage into freedom. A storm will spring up when our son rides into Thebes on his steed bridled with silver. And the people will dance and rejoice as they pray to a god newly arisen out of Dionysus and Apollo, fused into one by the power of freedom, a god of intoxication and reason, a god of life and death, a god of hate and a god of love.

"Princess, you must go now, it has been much more than a moment, and the helmet has slipped down over your eyes so that you cannot see anything. If the officer making the rounds finds you here, I cannot vouch either for you or for me." She awakens from the dream, takes off helmet and shield, descends into the town by way of the wooden stairs, the town waiting for war, and wends her way to the dismal palace.

I am on the Zeil, a busy shopping street. It is thronged with people out buying Christmas presents with grim determination. They are dressed well but without elan, and as each of them pushes his way along, he is surrounded by an aura of solitude, coldness, aloofness, aggression. I myself never succumbed to that postwar mania characteristic of so many emigrants that made them see a potential Nazi in every German and led them repeatedly to provoke unpleasant incidents. No taxi driver ever told me that everything was better under Hitler; no hairdresser ever complained about the injustice perpetrated by the Russians, the Czechs, and the Poles when they drove out the ethnic Germans; no fellow passenger in a train ever asserted that the tales about the concentration camps were filthy lies and that there was no truth to the claim that six million Jews were murdered. Since my return I have never felt afraid of the Germans, but in this crowd I am seized with irrational fear. Perhaps the fear in these people's faces is contagious—it is the fear of not being able to cope with a world turned inimical to human life. A very German fear? I do not think so, although in other countries, where people are more communicative, more neighborly, the fear is not so noticeable. The silence spreads and spreads, profound uneasiness at not being able to answer the question: Where are we bound?

He was here, came into the city without seeing his little sister. That would have given him away, so it had been arranged this way. He was here. The guards let him through, and he moved circumspectly, sword in hand, peering about him to make sure he had not been lured into a trap. He made his way to where he was to meet with Eteocles. Who rejected everything. Sharing the kingship was out of the question, that had not changed. He, Eteocles, would remain the sole ruler of Thebes, now and forever. If Polyneices wanted war, he could have it. And, with a provoking laugh, "You may not be aware of this, but Antigone is in Thebes. Should you and your men manage to breach one of the gates, which I do not believe you can, Antigone will die. Bear that in mind." The slave Leander was present at the meeting and reported verbatim what was said.

So: a hostage. If things go according to wish and Polyneices proves victorious, it will mean death. O Gods, grant him victory.

"Do you take cream?" A girl in a black dress and little pink apron is standing at my table, looking at me quizzically.

"No, thank you," I say, and I am not quite sure what I am saying no to. Then it dawns on me that I am sitting in the Kranzler Café, surrounded by middle-aged and elderly women with plates of eclairs, whipped-cream torte, and Danish pastries before them. A little gray poodle with a purple collar set with semiprecious stones begs demurely and is given a mouthful of cake. It eats the cake on the plush carpet under the table and begs again, receiving another mouthful.

Two young people enter, wearing jeans and leather jackets. The lady with the poodle jerks the dog's leash, pulling the animal close as if she had to protect it against murderers.

I smile at the young people, but they look right past me—I am just one of many, an old lady who sits around in cafés because she has nothing better to do. There is nothing to distinguish me from the crowd of dull bourgeois ladies frittering away their afternoon here.

Oedipus, who was not an intellectual but an intuitive genius, solved the riddle of the Sphinx. He did not say: the gods, God, the divine. He said: Man. Man as the measure, the basis, the material of all dialectics, Man as beginning and end. Anyone who does not recognize man's significance is eaten by the Sphinx. Many of the people sitting around me do not even notice that they were gobbled up long ago.

10

Fleeing home. Fleeing as a state of being, without my knowing what I am fleeing. Fleeing from the Nazis—now, those were the days; you had something real to be afraid of, were really running away, hiding, compelled to act, even if what you did was sometimes precisely the wrong thing, as in Waiki's case. But in the end I learned all the tricks for survival and became the ideal victim of persecution.

Still am. Yet no one is persecuting me now. I can come and go as I wish, use any mode of transportation, travel anywhere (almost); the passport in my handbag is authentic—German, in fact, which sometimes strikes me as odd or ridiculous—and yet I am still fleeing. Not from myself (that would be too simple an explanation), not from other people (actually, I seek them out), not from the world (my curiosity, my pathological craving for information). I am fleeing, borne by a force that hurtles my body forward when the car has long since crashed into a tree, a destructive force that drives me to flee toward death.

I open the door to my apartment and stop dead on the threshold: two coats that do not belong to me are hanging on the coatrack. I recognize one of them, a leather coat, as Christine's. She comes from the living room, looking paler than this morning, somehow edgy. "Forgive us for barging in here."

"Who is us?"

"A friend of mine, Marlene." Silence. "We'd like to . . ." Silence. "We wanted to ask whether it would be all right for her to stay here awhile, perhaps overnight."

"Why?"

"She doesn't know where else to go."

"Can't she go to a hotel?"

"No."

"Even if I pay for it?"

"No, she really can't."

I realize that this Marlene, whose real name is certainly not Marlene, is being sought by the police, and I ask no more questions. Even if I heard that she was a murderer—and I do not want to hear any such thing—I could not send her away. A fugitive does not turn away another fugitive.

As I hang up my coat, I find myself wishing this Marlene would turn out to be utterly charming. A typical young person's wish: You are about to meet someone new, and the thought crosses your mind that this person is going to be The One. The beautiful taut face of the young Marlene Dietrich flashes before me—I am yearning to fall in love, fearful that I am no longer capable of it.

We step into the room. Marlene is sitting at my desk, staring straight in front of her. She does not get up. She is smoking a cigarette, letting the ashes drop onto the floor. She is still almost a child, eighteen or nineteen. The sight of her fills me with sadness. "You can stay here," Christine tells her, although I have not actually given my permission. Marlene does not respond.

"I'm going to run along now. I'll try to arrange things so she'll be out of here soon."

"Don't do anything foolish." She looks at me with

amusement. I should not have said that. It was as silly as saying, "Drive carefully." I accompany her back to the hall, where I hold up my crossed fingers: "Good luck!" There, that was better.

"Everything is okay. I'm not involved in this."

"It is really serious?"

"For someone else, not for her. He was hiding out in her apartment, and they found him there. They didn't arrest her. Probably an oversight. Now she just has to lie low for a while. But don't worry, she's all right."

I smile at Christine. She kisses me. Puts on her coat and goes. Leaving me alone with this girl, about whom I know nothing.

I stand there in the hall. Take my clothes brush out of the shoe cabinet and brush my sweater, which does not need it. I am trying to think what all this might mean. Christine would not saddle me with a criminal. The girl probably has connections with terrorists, hid one of them in her apartment, is a sympathizer. A nasty, uninformative word. Does it apply to those who approve of murder, or does it mean those who attempt, as I do, to understand how helplessness can breed violence? I am not a sympathizer when it comes to murder, yet I may be considered one if they find Marlene here. They will not find her.

When I step back into the room I have the uneasy feeling that I have been had—I suspect Christine's definition of someone who is "all right" differs from mine. At the same time I am flattered by her trust.

Marlene is still sitting at the desk, using the chair I want for myself, the chair I always sit in when I am alone and when I have company. I do not ask her to relinquish it. Instead, I sit down on the sofa; I would prefer to lie down, but cannot do that with a stranger present. Feel mildly amused that someone is hiding out with me because she has hidden someone else and must now disappear. I know this game, it is simply that I had not thought of it for a long time.

I ask whether she would like anything to eat. She shakes her head, lights another cigarette. Nothing to be done. If she does not want to eat, it is no affair of mine. I fetch my own cigarettes from the desk. She has my lighter in her hand. I say, "Would you mind?" She pushes the lighter toward me with a mechanical gesture. She is probably suffering from shock. I have often seen people in a state of shock. All those who were brought into the Schouwburg. Unable to cry. Broken. I could do little for them. The only effective form of help: being there. Which was seldom possible in the rush and commotion of those nights. Now I have time. Can sit and wait. Withdraw to the sofa.

We smoke in silence. I have no idea whether she finds the silence as painful as I do. What could I talk about with her? Certainly not about the events that led to her being here. As children we used to play a game in which we would stare at each other, and the first one to make a face was the loser. I can bear it no longer. "Are you still in school?"

"No."

"Have you graduated?"

"Yes."

"Are you at the university?"

"I was."

"For how long?"

"A year."

"What were you studying?"

"Classical philology." So reluctant. As if this were an interrogation. Perhaps she has already been interrogated and is suffering from trauma. I light another cigarette from the one I am finishing. She adds, "I

110

know I'm pretty hard for an old woman to take. I told Christine that."

I say casually, "Sometimes a person just has to assume such burdens." Then I ask her in a friendlier tone of voice, "Wouldn't you like to lie down?"

"I'd rather sit."

I pull my feet up onto the sofa, supporting myself on my elbow. An excellent position for conversation—it allows you to gesticulate, to shift around. A miserable position if you are not talking. Your hand goes to sleep, your arm aches. I look at Marlene. She is sitting there pigeon-toed, her feet in worn brown oxfords. Jeans. A blouse with green, beige, and red checks, a dark blue cardigan. No jewelry. No makeup. Her nails without polish but nicely cared for. Her hands are slender and well formed. Dark, shiny hair, bangs. A finely chiseled nose, long lashes, brown eyes. But her childlike mouth has a hard twist to it. On the floor next to her a stuffed Pan Am bag.

She seems apathetic. How little you can read from a face. And how much you think you can read. Bitterness, pleasure, hatred, despair. How often and completely you can be mistaken.

In spite of which I begin to form an image from this face. I try to picture Marlene as a little girl. Not the child of working-class people, nor of rich people. Probably good in school. Intelligent. Even very intelligent. Did she run away from pressures that had become unbearable? Did she have trouble forming lasting relationships? Did she dread being too dependent? I invent various motivations. All of them spring from the same source: despair.

This generation of nonconformists, plagued by irrational fears, unreachable—or no longer reachable, for when did we ever make a serious attempt to reach out to them? A generation that gets on our nerves, a mirror in which we see ourselves, despite the distortion. A generation that refuses to let us assert that all is well with the world. In those rare moments when we can relax and feel contentment, they pounce, sarcastically destroying our complacency: Oh, no you don't; how can you accept such compromises!

I ask her, "What did you plan to do with your training in classics?"

"I wanted to teach." In Germany you have to be a card-carrying conformist before they will turn you loose on their children. Now, even if she manages to stay out of jail, she will have to give up that plan.

Silence. I try desperately to think of some topic with which to break it. No doubt she has read Sophocles in the original. It would be perfectly natural to mention my interest in Antigone. Yet I cannot allow myself to use my princess as a decoy.

The solidarity of the persecuted? I say hesitantly, "You know, of course, that I'm Jewish?"

"No, how should I know? And what's it to me?" Christine's technique—many of the young folk use this same technique, throwing people together without telling them anything about each other. It is a completely unfamiliar situation to me, but one not without appeal, to meet someone who does not have me pigeonholed.

"We emigrated to Holland. My husband was seized during a raid, shipped off to the concentration camp at Mauthausen and murdered there."

She is listening. Gazing at me with those intelligent eyes. Encouraging me to continue. "I received two letters from him. On lined paper with a black border and all kinds of instructions in small print that took up a good deal of the meager space he was permitted to use once a month for a letter. The fine print said, for instance, that no packages could be sent because the prisoners in protective custody could buy anything they needed right there in the camp. But you were allowed to send money."

"Protective custody?"

"My husband was good at conveying all sorts of messages in a kind of code. In his first letter he promised not to kill himself. Everything sounded almost hopeless. In the second letter, a month later, there was no longer a shred of hope."

"You don't know what actually happened?"

"No."

I get up, fetch from the shelf the Dutch book entitled *The Holocaust* and open it to the photograph of the rock quarry at Mauthausen with the Death Steps. I place the book before her. The photograph comes from the SS archives and shows an endless column of men in striped prisoners' garb bowed under the weight of blocks of stone in wooden hods.

Then I begin to read aloud to her. The first sentences are from Eugen Kogon's book, *The Theory and Practice of Hell:* "There were 148 steps leading down to the bottom of the pit, but they were not permitted to use these. They had to slide down the loose stones at the side. And even here many died or were severely injured." I continue, sight-translating the Dutch text: "Yet that was not considered sufficiently efficacious, even though the added hardship drove many to commit suicide the very first day. On the third day the guards opened fire on them with machine guns, and one day later a dozen of the Jews took each other by the hand and leaped into the quarry. Even that was not enough, for there were still some prisoners left. In addition, the civilian employees at Mauthausen found this jumping (they called it 'parachute jumping') distasteful, because splatters of brain and flesh clung to the rocks, a disgusting sight. To spare these sensitive souls, about one hundred Jews were placed under the supervision of two executioners, one of whom was nicknamed 'Miss Blondie,' the other 'Killer Hans.' They specialized in the killing of Jews. We will not described what ensued. Three months later there was hardly anyone left. The reader should be under no illusions: this is not a complete account. Paul Tillard and other eyewitnesses saw more, a great deal more. This was Mauthausen, after all, with a commandant who gave his son as a birthday present fifty Jews to shoot down. This was Mauthausen, specifically set up for these atrocities, for this sort of death.''

She stares at the picture. Slowly she raises her hand, tightens it into a fist, and brings it down repeatedly on the book: ''Pigs! Pigs!''

I stroke her head. She jerks away and asks abruptly, ''Have you ever seen a person beaten?''

I have never seen that. I have seen it thousands of times. During the months Waiki was in Mauthausen I was beaten night after night. I have never been beaten. ''No, I never have.''

Every fiber in me goes taut, on the defensive: Don't say any more, leave me in peace, stop, don't open my wound; and who are you?—you just blew in here uninvited, a little girl who sympathizes with crazies, people hopelessly on the wrong track. You mean nothing to me. You are in my way. I have gone to a good deal of trouble to rebuild my life, shoring it up with compromises, taking up where I left off before the war, and I am still the daughter of a good, solid family, still a bleeding-heart liberal. I understand you, understand everyone, even wrote a story in which I identify with an SS man, for both of us are survivors, both of us are guilty. I went to Mauthausen with Urs, who was not very good at being a shoulder

114

to cry on, but was a comfort anyway. I took my comfort along, rather than try to face the situation alone. I was in the camp, not in the stone quarry, but even so I turned and fled after a few hellish minutes. Continued on to Vienna, went to the Opera, to the Royal Theater, where an elderly usher wished us "much edification," to Schönbrunn Palace, to the Albertina, the Spanish Riding School, and all those places one goes to as a tourist out to savor the delights of a place. My superficial life, my hedonistic life, twelve years wiped from the slate as though nothing had happened—Mauthausen never happened, for how could I even breathe if it had. Make love, not war. Twist Antigone's ambiguous statement, the statement that brought about her death, misuse it in the name of life. Excuses, excuses.

I hate Marlene. She has her head down on the photograph now and is sobbing. I love her.

11

I let her sob. I lie on the sofa—after all—and stare up at the ceiling. It is dingy. I should have it painted. Am filled with uneasiness, with fear. Fear of those who are hunting for this girl. Fear of the girl, whom I cannot help. When I returned to Germany, I boasted about the cyanide tablet in my pocketbook, if only to prove to my Jewish friends, who thought my returning showed lack of principle, that I was ready for all eventualities. Expecting the worst but hoping to escape it, I gradually began to think the Germans were capable of adjusting to democracy. Things went well, very well, in fact; I was living in a free country, where I could say what I thought and do what I wished. Years later I went out into the woods, dug a deep hole and buried the poison.

For some time now little flames have been flickering on the site of a fire that must have been smoldering unnoticed for a long while. Not a large fire. But the lighting has changed, as in the theater when a turn in the action is about to occur.

I am composing a letter in my head: Dear Gabi, All I know about you is your first name and that you are a sixteen-year-old student at a secondary modern school, or were one, rather, for considerable time has elapsed since you committed that statement of yours to paper. It was published along with those of many of your contemporaries, the idea being to show how little you young people knew about our recent past. Among those statements were many foolish and grotesquely misinformed ones; one could laugh or cry at them, as the case might be. But your statement stood out: it was concise, to the point, and tremendously moving. You said simply: "Hitler destroyed human beings."

For the first time it became clear to me that I had let myself be destroyed. It was not all Hitler's fault. It takes two for something like that, one to do it and the other to accept it. He promulgated insane laws, and I obeyed them. How could I take myself seriously if I argued that as a Jew I had no choice? I did not say no. Saying no is the only freedom that cannot be taken from you. Antigone made superb use of it. I said yes. Yes, I shall leave Germany, yes, I am no longer a German, yes, I shall give up my writing, yes, I shall wear the yellow star, yes, I shall type letters in that vile Schouwburg, yes, I shall make no effort to spring Waiki from the concentration camp, yes, I shall answer to a name that is not my own, yes, I shall not shoot the SS captain. In this way I shall save my life while destroying myself. If something has been destroyed, neither magic nor divine mercy can bring it back to life.

I have composed many letters in my head that were never written. I returned from Holland with every intention of taking an active role in public life. Nothing came of it. I did not even tell people that I was a survivor, a witness. I was appointed to no committees, invited to no panel discussions. I not only vote Social Democratic, I belong to the party, yet I never open my mouth at a meeting. I did not join forces with other writers, never tried to get into the Group 47, which included Germany's most promising postwar writers, did not lift a finger. I had no colleagues as acquaintances, only musicians and theater people, whom I met through Urs. Whenever possible I avoided saying I was a writer. I wrote under Waiki's name and lived under Urs's. Concealment came easily, and gradually I perfected my method. Why all the concealment?

The lingering effects of my upbringing. An attitude never articulated, merely demonstrated: Do not reveal yourself. Do not bare your soul. Sex is taboo. Putting yourself on display is taboo. It is vulgar to be too open.

Surrounding love with secrecy made the whole thing more thrilling. We wore magic cloaks that rendered us invisible, except to the beloved.

Every morning I would call my blond boyfriend Hans on the telephone to wake him. I had to be very careful to avoid being caught. Before going to our afternoon rendezvous, I would invent all sorts of explanations about visiting girl friends, seeing movies, taking bicycle trips. My parents did not even know a Hans existed. Possibly they would have had no objection. But I wanted to have this Hans, and other Hanses as well, entirely to myself.

Perhaps my reluctance to admit I am a writer has its origins here.

My timidity about facing the public has a basis in reality: my poor hearing. I have difficulty following discussions, and I hate to be saying constantly, "Pardon me?" and "What was that?" and "I did not catch what you said," let alone "My hearing is poor, could you please speak more distinctly," because the person I am talking with always confuses distinctly with loudly and begins to shout. Then I feel I am being yelled at, start to panic. My ears go on strike, and I cannot hear anything at all.

Marlene is still sobbing, but more quietly now, sounding resigned.

Another letter begins to take shape in my mind: Dear Mother, Now that you are dead, I can write to you. When you were living I could not bring myself to say anything. Did not even attempt to talk to you. I knew you were stronger than I.

I loved you and hated you. You got on my nerves, but sometimes I could hardly wait to be with you again. You reproached me with spoiling years of your life with my "misdemeanors." They were merely my reaction to the fact that you always seemed to hold it against me that I was not as pretty and gentle as the sister who died.

You and Father never quarreled. As a child I thus believed that a marriage was the communal life of two persons who never quarreled. Not until later, when I came to understand that conflict is an essential part of living together, did I realize how Father's stoic calm must have irritated you. Your high-strung nature bounced off him, this man whose well-being depended on knowing that everything he called his own—his wife, his children, his law practice—was in immaculate order. You took out your irritation on me, not on my brother, for he was a man, and for your generation that meant a superior being.

You were the kind of person one could count on in any scrape, but you lacked the tenderness I was longing for. Once when I was sixteen your cool manner put me in such a rage that I smashed a glass on your plate—only at the last moment did something stop me from throwing it at your head. And a few years later I ordered you out of your own car somewhere on a highway, then drove off. You had ambitions for me, wanted me to be a woman of the world, clever and desirable, yet in actuality you never expected me to succeed, either with people or in my profession. Your hands in a choke-hold around my neck. The most hurtful thing you ever said to me: that I was not competent to raise a child.

You were astonished and delighted when Waiki became your son-in-law. You were very fond of him, and mourned for him as if he had been your own child. You did not much like Urs, but you accepted him. He was an artist, after all, with an aristocrat for a mother.

You never noticed that I had a talent for writing, but even if you had, you would not have known how to nurture it. You were superficial in the grand manner, and I was astonished at your ability to glide over any abyss without a breath of anxiety.

All in all you were a good mother. Probably there are not many better. The mother–daughter relationship: full of pitfalls. Dependency that breeds hatred. A permanent guilty conscience. You were perfectly right when you said I was not competent to raise a child. I would not have been. No one is. The same mistakes, committed again and again, over the centuries, down through the generations.

I often long for you. Wish I were sick, so you could nurse me. Wish my bathroom had your clean, fresh smell. Wish I could listen to your small talk, your witty running commentary on life. And wish you were here so that I could tell you that today a girl was brought to me in despair. What can I do to help her?

You have already cooked dinner for Marlene? Made up a bed for her? Put the sleeping pills on the bedside table? You are sure she will calm down soon? And what if she does not? What if the wound stays with her all her life? Like mine? You did not know I had a wound? Did you never smell the stench of the pus? Notice the blood-soaked bandages? You do not know what I am talking about? I should not get so worked up? You say I should take off my blouse and scrub out the tomato sauce I splattered on it? That I should not smoke in the kitchen while I am doing the dishes? This afternoon I am to take you to see the princess and must not forget to buy flowers for her and dog biscuits for the snarling bulldog? And tomorrow we go first to the cemetery, to the grave of my pretty, well-behaved sister, where Father is buried too now, and then we take a walk through the English Garden, and then we visit Frau So-and-So, and then we go to a movie?

But tomorrow I mean to do some writing, Mother dear; otherwise, my Antigone will never be finished. I see, you think that is not so important, and the day after tomorrow will be another day?

That was the pattern when we were together, and I always gave in. For years. You reached a ripe old age. And when your choking hands released my neck, I was still giving in. That part of me that is you.

The letter has tired me out. Longing for my mother has returned. Also my guilty conscience. I saw her through the war, saved her from Auschwitz. But in her last years I should have spent more time with her. And when I did spend time with her, I should have done so less grudgingly. Without always glancing at my watch and wishing she would stop telling me about people in whom I had no interest.

And then hastily, frantically, as though I were afraid my strength would fail me, another letter: Dear Friedel, Not long ago your brother was sorting out old letters and came upon your manuscript describing the liquidation of the ghetto in the Polish town of Piotrkow, in German called Petrikau. He brought it to me. Typed on wartime paper, yellowed and crumbling. I have to pick it up very carefully, or it might fall to pieces in my hands.

Your brother often spoke of you. You were only a couple of years older than I, an intellectual and a man of the theater, who had gone to the famous Odenwald School and was, as we all were in those days, a pacifist and a leftist. We never met, but I am sure we had many acquaintances in common, for we belonged to the same circles. Neither you nor I was trained in obedience, but on the other hand no one has taught us to be wary of slogans, either. And so we allowed ourselves to be destroyed, you as a German soldier, I as one of the persecuted.

You lived for years with a Jewish woman. I met your pretty, intelligent girl friend in Holland, before she was captured while attempting to escape and was shipped off to the East.

You yourself never returned from the front. Your life came to an end in January '45 somewhere in Poland. The circumstances are unknown.

But before that you had been sent to Piotrkow. You recorded in writing what took place there, probably in order to preserve your sanity. Your testament. For your children, for me, for all of us.

The Jews were loaded onto a truck, the old people helped up with kicks, the children tossed as if they were parcels. The truck drove to the cemetery and returned empty. All day long.

At times your sober language becomes emotional. Describing women waiting to be taken away, you write: "Actually they all have the same look in their eyes. For a moment I think: All these women and girls are standing there dreaming."

It was not only the women who were dreaming; you were, too. Dreaming the worst dream of your life, witnessing the slaughter of your beloved, seeing your two little children pitched onto the truck. You stood by, motionless, one of the murderers.

And I am standing next to you, dreaming like you, knowing that I am dreaming, unable to wake up, unwilling to wake up, because I sense that behind the glassy rigidity of the dream something else awaits me: reality, even more brutal. Now and again we look at each other and immediately lower our eyes: an admission of failure.

I am standing on the truck that goes to the cemetery. I do not protest, do not shout, am surprised that I do not protest, that I do not shout, that I am a puppet that simply accepts everything. Puppets that murder, puppets that allow themselves to be murdered, in this dream at world's end, this dream you have flung over me, a deadly, poisoned mesh in which I am entangled for all eternity.

12

Walking across the great hall, coldly magnificent. Toward the table, summoned to an audience. An interminable advance toward the center of power, a pale oval, the small head perched atop a tall, gaunt body, a faceless head that decides who shall live, who shall die.

Walking with a spring in the step, shoulders back, toes turned out and touching down before the heels—the trained gait of a princess; it was abandoned during the journey through the mountains, but on marble pavement the body reverts to the old patterns.

No sound but the gentle *clip-clop* of sandals. Silence as the cornerstone of fear. Thou shalt fear. An artificial desert, nothing to see, nothing to hear. The oval hovers in the distance, inaccessible.

Every day at mealtimes there is the uncle's face, not loved, no, but trusted. The small wart on the left, above his upper lip; eyes without lashes; bald head. His mouth handsomely curved, intelligent. Creon says little, occasionally makes a bit of a joke, at which everyone laughs, although it is seldom funny. The desert has swallowed up that face, leaving an empty oval, the most fearful of images.

Closer, ever closer. Just before the table, the right leg should swing backward in a semicircle, while the left knee bends. The position should be held until Creon's hand points to a chair.

Sitting down, waiting. Interminably. A demonstration of how power can do as it wishes with time.

Then the voice. Very soft. More tentative, groping than commanding.

He reaches far back into the past. Dwells on the family history, reveals how he despised Laius and Oedipus. The grandfather dissipated, the father reckless. Both of them irresponsible, obsessed with power and pleasure. Not statesmen. Polyneices their worthy successor. Prepared to destroy Thebes to satisfy his ambition and lust for power.

"Inconceivable what would happen if I did not keep order. The people want a firm hand on the helm. The body social can survive only if the welfare of the state is placed before that of the individual. Eteocles, the king, still needs guidance. Haemon—I would have liked him to turn out differently. Hangs around home, studying history instead of making it himself. I admit it was I who suggested he write up the story, for it seemed important to me that the grandchildren should learn about what took place, but I could not have anticipated Haemon's going overboard this way. Nothing to be done, you cannot change human beings.

"Ismene, blond, pale, characterless. Someday she will marry a prince from abroad. Then she will be out of the way. That leaves only one—Antigone. Niece and daughter-in-law. Burdened with a terrible heritage. Which she seems to have overcome, or merely conceals skillfully. Is she as intelligent as she appears? As sly as I suspect? I do not know what to make of her.

"Sometimes I think she is stupid, despite her intelligence. Taking Polyneices' side. No need to inter-

126

rupt, I know all about it. But she is playing a dangerous game, one I wish to put a stop to. I forbid her to continue roaming through the city. A princess must not be on such easy terms with the populace. Instead, she will devote herself to the work that a war demands of the king's sister. Tending the wounded, distributing food, raising morale. All with the proper aloofness that preserves the aura of divine origin.

"I did not want this war. But I shall bear up better under it than Polyneices. He has too much imagination and too little common sense. Imagination is fine for solving riddles—and for plunging entire peoples into tragedy."

The right hand rises and catches the slowly sinking oval, which gradually fills with the uncle's features, the weary face of an old man. Battered, in color and texture like dry, cracked clay. Already almost earth, which it will soon be.

This is not how monsters look. Conscientious councilmen, successful traders look like this, decent folk who find imagination irritating and are suspicious of anyone who dares to be different. They want no changes. The gods have decreed how things are to be, now and forever.

"She and Polyneices hate me, I know that. She should not shake her head, it is so. Has been since they were children. Why?"

When no reply comes, he continues, speaking even more softly than before.

"I am sorry for her. Even if I do not understand her, I am fond of her. Of all the children, she is the dearest to me. It would be painful to have to destroy her. I hope things do not reach that point. If for no other reason than that a woman does not count. But she should not think I will spare her if she opposes me."

127

The naked lids are lowered, shielding the enormity of this admission of affection. His mouth smiles ironically, as if to take back everything just uttered.

Then his hand gestures to indicate the audience is over.

Marlene is leaning back in my chair, her eyes closed. I ask whether there is anything I can do for her. No reply. Don't mess up your life, there is still time, you haven't gone over the brink yet, but the day is not far off when you will, and then there will be no retreating. Those are my thoughts. I do not speak them, and am filled with the devastating sense of standing next to a person bleeding to death and being incapable of lifting a finger.

How would I have behaved that night when Antigone went over the brink, had I been with her? Would I have said: Don't go out of the city, leave Polyneices to his own devices, this is not a good enough reason for sacrificing your life?

Approximately the same advice you would receive from a counselor on a crisis hotline who has only a small repertoire of options? Yet his chances of hitting on the right one are considerable, because anyone who will turn to a complete stranger in his hour of need really wants to be helped.

Antigone had no other aim than to bury Polyneices. One may call her behavior hysterical or compulsive, and psychiatry probably has a few other labels for an act so extraordinarily single-minded and unreasonable.

The sudden insight that my princess has much in common with Marlene and would be just as difficult to put up with. The thought is painful. I surmise that the flesh-and-blood Antigone, not the one I can call forth and send back into obscurity at will, would put quite a strain on my nerves. My horror of irrational people. I have never gone over the brink, have always compromised, like all those who do not take morality so seriously. We healthy, realistic souls whom the gods do not rob of our wits.

An evening in Amsterdam, June 11, 1941, with daylight gently fading. I am standing at the window, looking into the great expanse of sky, and slowly the truth is borne in upon me: Waiki has not turned up in either of the two apartments available to him as hideouts; he must have fallen into the hands of the Gestapo. Pain begins to pierce me, the pain that will never again leave me, with which I shall have to live, and as if someone else were speaking, I say to myself: I wish it were all over. I say it to my mother, sitting small and miserable in the room behind me. She gets up, comes over to me, and tries to caress me, where-upon I begin to scream as if she had struck me. At that moment I must seem crazed to her. I am crazed; I beg her with my eyes: Give me a torch so I can set the world on fire. I want everyone to perish. I want to destroy everything, but I do not go over the brink—I do not have it in me, and even in my madness I hold on to a shred of rationality that helps me grope my way from one support to the next. The desire to destroy the world is impossible to fulfill; Antigone's desire was not at all unfulfillable: she could bury Polyneices.

That evening no one showed me a photograph of the Death Steps, but I needed no picture to guess what would happen. I had a vivid imagination and knew what human beings were capable of. I had grasped what a concentration camp was all about long before I was directly affected, but now Hitler had become a personal enemy. He had had it in for Waiki from the outset, not as a Jew but as an intellectual and a political opponent; by standing reality on its head

129

this way, I gave my hatred a specific target. In that period, while my beloved was being tortured to death and I was longing to die, I must have been filled with an uncanny life force. Uncanny to me at the time, as it is today.

13

Marlene is speaking. So quietly that I cannot make out what she is saying. At first I think she has asked for something. But that cannot be, for she continues to speak, quickly, agitatedly, without pausing, without looking at me. Never mind my ears—I turn up the hearing aid to top volume, but to no avail.

I break in: "I'm hard of hearing, couldn't you speak a little more distinctly?"

Her hunted eyes. Almost a shout: "No, I can't!" And on she goes, still mumbling.

My daily torment. Intensified this time by the certainty that it would be terribly important to find out something about her. That she may be saying things she will never say again. I get up from the sofa, hitch myself up on the edge of the desk; at this distance I should be able to hear her. But she has stopped speaking. Shakes her head irritably and remains silent.

I am hurt, paralyzed, sit there on the desk and do not know how I will ever escape from this perch. Leaden exhaustion, a wall between Marlene and me, a wall between the world and me, leaving me cut off, isolated. I pass my hand over the wooden surface as a dying person brushes over the bedclothes. Feel a surge of resentment, against myself, against Marlene.

The bell rings. With great relief I slide off the desk.

Marlene jumps up, makes a grab for me, and holds on to my arm. "You are not to open the door. I won't let you open the door."

"Of course I intend to open the door."

A moment of intense hostility. She says, "Christine has a key. My friends don't ring."

"Well, mine do."

"You were expecting someone?"

"No." The bell rings again. Now she has both arms around me; I try to shake her off, without success. We remain locked together.

The more hysterical she gets, the calmer I become. Then I remember Herr Schieding. "That must be my tax consultant."

"Are you sure?"

"Quite sure." Resigned, she releases me. "Now, you go into my bedroom and stay there quietly until we're alone again." She obeys like a well-behaved child. I say, "Lie down for a bit," and close the door, press the button that opens the lobby door and step out into the hall. I hear someone coming in downstairs.

While the elevator descends and comes up again, I play the old what-if game: Suppose it really is the police? What are the charges against Marlene? How urgently are they looking for her? What is the proper way for me to behave, in view of the fact that I know nothing about this case? Her coat is on my coatrack (it is much too long to be mine). The room is full of smoke. The ashtray contains butts both with and without filters. What explanation could I give if they noticed that particular detail? They must not have an opportunity to notice it, must not enter the apartment. What, a stranger in my apartment? You're mistaken, gentlemen, I am here alone, writing. Yes, I'm a writer. Are you interrupting my work? Well, actually you are, but I know you are only doing your duty. It is reassuring for a citizen to discover we are being so well protected. These days, what with the shocking increase in crime. All this in a creaky voice. In between the sentences, wheezing breaths. Sounds like emphysema, or asthma, certainly something serious, and these are no doctors. That is the best bet, my feeble-old-lady pose. I am good at it, use it now where I once assumed my shy-young-girl or flustered-housewife roles, which seldom failed to achieve the desired effect.

But perhaps I shall not have the time to play my role. What if they open fire from the elevator? The idea tickles me. Finished off by a German in uniform after all. Many years too late, a joke whose point will be lost on the audience.

But of course it is Herr Schieding. His round face beams at me. "To be quite honest, I'm glad you don't have your dog anymore. I was petrified of him."

I think: He might just as well have said: I'm glad you don't have your husband anymore. He was so standoffish. (Urs was standoffish; he was never on good terms with money or people who dealt with it.) But that is not what Herr Schieding says. He is too well brought up for that. Where a dog is involved, he need not conceal his feelings or show consideration for mine. He takes off his dark overcoat, props his umbrella against the shoe cabinet, having noted with chagrin that there is no umbrella stand, and adjusts his silver-gray tie before the mirror. His dress suggests that he wishes to resemble a London banker, but he is and will always be a German accountant, no matter how he tries.

At the door to the smoke-filled living room, he draws back in horror. "Goodness, how can you smoke so much when it's so bad for you!" I open the window, remove the ashtrays, return with sherry, glasses, and a plate of cookies, close the window again, and sit down at my desk, while he draws up a chair.

He officiously fetches a file out of his briefcase and takes out papers, which he spreads out on the desk. How does he ever get any work done, if everything takes him so long? I drum impatiently on the desk. But he calmly begins to lecture me, not only about my taxes and all the tricks I should use so as to pay as little as possible, but also about my stocks, some of which I should unload "in light of the general situation." He has picked up a little Tibetan tea bowl made of dark wood lined in a silver alloy, and is holding it, turning it back and forth as he drones on in his soporific Frankfurt dialect, expressing his confidence that these stocks will fall and others will gain in value. "Get rid of them," he orders me, "and buy fixed-interest instruments—you'll be better off. At your age—" He stops suddenly, appalled at what he has just said, then forges bravely ahead. "Excuse me for saying this, but at your age a person has no business speculating anymore. You should get as much as you can in immediate return, and spend it, too. You have no children, so tell me, whom would you want to be saving for? The government will just take it. . . ."

If Hitler had not come along, would I have had children? Probably. Does an old person whose children have left the nest feel more protected? At least there is someone to think about, to worry about. Worry over the children—it provides the principal content of so many parents' lives, a substitute for their own, which are becoming increasingly empty.

I am studying in Berlin, have just had a long debate about Marxism with a male friend. He sees me back to my place on Olivaer Platz. Having had my fill

134

of intellectual effort, I wait just inside my door until he is gone, then take a taxi to a Lesbian café on Uhlandstrasse.

All I am after is relaxation, and I can relax better dancing with women than with men, who always assume you are out to entrap them. I sit down at a little table, order a gin fizz, and look over the clientele. Most of them I know by sight, but one woman whom I have not seen here before stands out because of her unusual beauty. Like most of the others, she is dressed in a man's suit, and has close-cropped hair, but in contrast to the others she wears no makeup. Nor does she need any. Makeup would only spoil the slanting gray eyes, the large, sensitive mouth. When I have stared at her long enough, she smiles, comes over to my table, and asks whether I would like to dance. Not until we get onto the floor and she takes the lead, do I notice her broad, hairy wrists and realize she is a man. A man who wishes he were a woman and seeks out the company of Lesbians because he feels more like them than like other women. We dance together many times in the course of the evening, and then he walks me home. On the way he tells me he belongs to the SA. That takes me completely by surprise; I am shocked, but also a bit amused that one of the Führer's soldiers should be trotting along beside me so gallantly. ''I'm Jewish,'' I say to provoke him, but he merely laughs: ''Politics don't interest me, and I have nothing against Jews. I just like wearing the uniform. I makes me feel like somebody.'' I understand his motivation perfectly: if he cannot be a woman, at least he can cut a fine figure. Playing soldier: occupational therapy for the unemployed. When he embraces me at the door, I am overwhelmed by his physical attractiveness and draw him into my room. We make love. He is a tender lover. We do not talk much, either this first night or during the ones that follow. We have few topics in common. For three weeks we are in love and blissful, until I decide that enough is enough and leave town without telling him. That is the end of the affair.

Back home in Munich at my parents' I discover that I am pregnant. I am yearning for a child and seriously consider letting nature take its course. But what would I say if the child asked about its father? Of course, I could make up a father, a man with splendid qualities who died, but I do not want to lie to my child. And to admit that he was a Nazi, no matter what his reasons, is impossible. So: no child.

Perhaps it would have been murdered in Auschwitz. . . .

But one should not embroider such titillating stories too much. Tabloid-style glimpses of Germany before Hitler's seizure of power. With a piquant dash of decadence, for which Berlin was famous in that period, and rumblings of the threat that hung over the country. An episode—nothing more, nothing less.

Herr Schieding is still fixated on his bowl, still talking. He does not notice that I have stopped listening, am somewhere else. He does not look at me, but sits there with a beatific smile, so sure of himself and all his accumulated wisdom.

I think uneasily of Marlene. Why did I not send him away, telling him that today was not good because I had to nurse someone who was very sick? The plain truth, and yet I could not bring myself to say the words. The compulsion to keep an appointment, whatever the cost.

''Why don't you make some money under the counter? It's the easiest thing. You buy instruments at the bank and put them in a safe-deposit box. Not at your bank—at one you don't do business with. Once a year you tuck a pair of scissors in your pocket, go to the bank, and clip the coupons.''

In my photographic studio I am watching three men pack up my furniture, equipment, lamps, chemicals, and paper. It was all inventoried months ago, and now everything I need for my work is being carted away. On orders from the ''Central Office for Jewish Emigration,'' the studio is closed from today on. A fourth man, the supervisor, has a master list on which he checks off every object as the others drop it into a crate or haul it away. ''A pair of scissors is missing,'' he says finally. ''Where are they?''

''I don't know.'' I know perfectly well that they are in the kitchen drawer. But speechless with indignation, I refuse to submit anymore, refuse to run and fetch when someone whistles.

''It is very stupid of you to want to be shipped off to Poland, all for a pair of scissors.'' I do not want to be shipped off to Poland, but there is nothing I can do if he wants to send me there. He shakes his head disapprovingly: ''I'm going to go and get a cup of coffee. You have twenty minutes to remember where you put the scissors.''

Scissors, scissors, scissors. Snipping my life in two. Scissors, scissors . . . I am humming a little song. Suddenly I perceive how meaningless my resistance is. I fetch the scissors from the kitchen, take them into my workroom, where the least disagreeable of the men is nailing up the last crate. ''I found them.''

''No, Mevrouw, I found them, not you,'' says the devil's packer, a ''good'' Dutchman. He takes the scissors from me and holds them up: ''Here, under the excelsior.'' When the gangster boss returns, everything is taken care of. At the door the packer turns to

137

me once more: "Things won't always be this way, Mevrouw."

Apparently Herr Schieding has finished his explanations. He has replaced the tea bowl on the desk, and now he pushes the tax return toward me, pointing with his index finger to the line he has marked with an X: "Please sign here."

"Sign here," says the man behind the window at the Central Office, and pushes a form toward me. I sign. He snatches back the document, glances at it, and rips it up. Menacingly: "I could have you sent away for that." All at once I understand. I sign the next form he hands me with "Sarah" in front of my own name. Every Jewish woman is called Sarah, every Jewish man Israel.

I begin with a large S, stop in horror and cross it out, then sign the tax return and give it to Herr Schieding. "Well, that does it," he says, gathers up his papers, stows them away in his briefcase, stands up, and is suddenly in a hurry to be gone.

When he has left, I return to the living room, sink into my chair, take the tea bowl, which rests lightly in my palm, and slowly turn it in a circle to see it glow, go dull, glow, and go dull. Birth, death, birth, death. Beginning of life, end of life, a pattern I can no longer accept. Perhaps I never could and always had to start from scratch, but earlier I was sustained by anticipation, curiosity, confidence. All that is gone now. I no longer stand firmly on the earth. I hover in uncertainty. Without joy, without despair I let myself drift.

14

I go in to Marlene. She is asleep on my bed, her right hand pressed to her mouth. She might lie this way on a meadow, in a man's arms, wherever a bit of happiness is to be found.

I cautiously sit down on the edge of the bed. She looks lovely, tranquil and contented. But the moment she wakes up, the pain will return, harsher, more piercing than before.

When Waiki is in Mauthausen, I am afraid of going to sleep, because at bedtime fear of waking up grips me. I wander restlessly through the apartment, which now seems meaningless—everything has become meaningless, the whole world is meaningless. Again and again I pass the gray-flecked coat that he did not take with him that evening in June and that I have kept on the coatrack. To put it away would be an admission I do not believe Waiki will return, and although I do not believe he will, I cannot admit it. I have the feeling that I will be killing him the instant I take the coat off its hanger. And so I press my face into the coarse material, which smells of him, his skin, his soap, his pipe tobacco. Am I crazy? A madwoman is roaming through our apartment, opening and closing doors, turning lights on and off, doing all those things people do every day. If I were still sane, I would burn the coat in my garbage pail; the day after the Germans marched into Holland I spent hours burning papers in that pail: letters from friends, émigré newspapers, leftist books. Burn the coat, pour gasoline over myself, set myself alight. Immolation of widows makes perfect sense.

Sometimes I stand at the window. When I count more women than men among the first twenty passers-by, I tell myself everything will turn out all right. But then three children come along, and from above I cannot be sure whether they are boys or girls, nor do I know whether I ought to include children. So I begin again from the beginning. I manipulate the quota: in the morning, when people are on their way to work, there are supposed to be more men, and a few hours later, when the housewives go shopping, more women. An idiotic game, I know, and yet I refuse to stop playing it. It has become a compulsion, because I cannot bear the silence around me. When a few people make timid attempts to comfort me, it is as if they were pricking their fingers to give a few drops of blood to keep alive someone dying of thirst.

In my godforsaken condition I go to see a palmist. He jabbers away, cleverly worming information out of me, but not so cleverly that I do not see through him. I feed him a series of false leads, which he gratefully follows up, a first-class idiot. He does not even guess my profession correctly, something any child could do on the basis of the brown stains left on my fingers by the developer. At the end he feels obligated to say something encouraging, to give me my money's worth: "Your husband is coming in October." In October news of Waiki's death arrives. Every morning I fetch my mail from the box downstairs, but on this particular day another tenant has already met the postman and shoved the letter under my door. I pick it up; it is my last letter to Waiki, stamped RETURN TO

SENDER. Above that someone has scrawled in red ink, *Addressee unknown.* So Waiki is unknown in Mauthausen; when I last heard, he was still there, and now his name is no longer recognized. Gradually, very gradually, despair mounts in me. I want, before it overwhelms me completely, to take the pills I procured the day after his arrest. But I cannot bring myself to do that; perhaps I am mistaken, perhaps he has merely been transferred to another block or another camp. Perhaps, perhaps. Not until two weeks later do I receive official notification through the Jewish Council, final certainty.

In October Urs arrives; it is the last time during the war that he visits me. We do not see each other until five years later, and then we stay together. The palmist's oracle was as ambiguous as the Pythian sibyl's.

I go on living, waking up every morning, going to sleep every night. Every morning, every night. For so many years. Sentenced to losing Waiki bit by bit. First no longer remembering his voice, then forgetting his smell, finally needing a photograph to help me recall what he looked like. But the picture shows him as a young man, who might be my son, and eventually my grandson. I dream I have my grandson as a lover, and cry myself to sleep. All that remains to me of Waiki is my wound, pain born of the pain I have lost, my most profound reality.

I wear the yellow star on my coat. Conceived as a humiliation, it makes us proud; what others dare only whisper, we have license to proclaim out loud: that we do not belong to the murderers.

I wear the yellow star on my coat. Am one of the chosen, as we have been from time immemorial, for good and for ill. But I also have the same longing we have had from time immemorial to be one of the

141

many, the ordinary people, neither murderers nor victims.

I weep. Waiki cannot weep, he is much too agitated. Dutch SA troops have just carried out a raid on the Jewish quarter, whose occupants resisted, killing one Nazi. In retribution they have sent four hundred young Jewish men to a concentration camp. Waiki is young, one of those in greatest danger. We know we ought to do something, but are paralyzed. We ought to, ought to . . . The hopelessness of our situation. No prospects whatsoever. And then the dockworkers stage a sympathy strike. Others follow, and a general strike develops, lasting two full days. The Germans are astonished at such a display of solidarity and do little to squelch it. A wave of enthusiasm sweeps us. We are not alone. The Dutch are sticking by us. The enthusiasm ebbs. Next time there will be no strike. Four months later, when the second roundup of young Jewish men takes place, Waiki is among them.

"You were in hiding?" people ask me when I return to Germany. "How nice that you survived the war." They are happy that I am still alive. On the scale of their conscience, one live Jew outweighs many thousands of dead Jews.

A department store goes up in flames one night. The fire is quickly extinguished. A few young people, from good middle-class backgrounds, announce they set the fire to protest the war in Vietnam. To give people a taste of what was going on there.

The onset of terrorism in Germany. A despairing reaction to pervasive inhumanity. Antigone and Gudrun Ensslin as ideological bedfellows. The noblest of virgins and this girl who is dismissed as a criminal. What is the difference? Is it merely that Antigone lived so long ago? I try to side with my princess. She set nothing on fire, she merely buried the dead. But that is not enough to differentiate the two; perhaps Gudrun, a minister's daughter, would have preferred to bury someone, if it were still possible nowadays to champion a principle by burying a corpse. Both of them acted out of moral fervor.

And what about me? I have spent the better part of a lifetime just licking my wound. Played Russian roulette with a nonexistent pistol. Merely fantasized about fire. No real attempt to destroy myself, no attempt to mount a public demonstration. The responsibility for my mother. The responsibility every individual Jew bears for all other Jews. Truth and excuses. And what *is* the truth in this incomprehensible, preprogrammed world, for which we all bear the responsibility? I see all this terribly clearly, but now I have the excuse that I am too old to change anything, so I simply lick my wound.

When does one really become too old? At what point do people start adding that lethal little ''still'' to everything one does? Ah, so you still ski, still drive a car, still go mountain-climbing, still take long trips, can still read without glasses, still do your own housework, can still be asked to do things for others. You can still think, still react like a normal human being, are still not a complete psychic and physical cripple, still think yourself capable of love, still want to be listened to—it's wonderful that you still live like a young person, but just wait and see: tomorrow, or the day after at the very latest, all that will change. These remarks are not intended as a respectful *memento mori*; they are spiteful, intended to undermine one's confidence, and they constitute a never-ending source of dread for me. Perhaps Marlene thinks of me not only in light of this litany of ''still's'' but also in light of another hostile image that hurts me acutely: old woman with money. Perhaps she also thinks: Dear old thing.

Or: That's how I would like to be when I'm old. Perhaps she brushes off any gestures of affection only because she hungers for them, longs for the support of an experienced person who no longer views things so emotionally.

Once again I feel the kind, ample bosom of the Hungarian doctor, Manzi, in which I bury my head for protection when my mother comes into the room and announces that Waiki's name is on the list of the dead. I am not the sort of young girl who treats the elderly with tenderness. I hate my grandmother, want to kill her, and her friends, all of whom I consider superannuated. Even my own father, who I wish would live forever, if only for my sake, I dismiss with a shrug when he says he cannot see anything in Expressionism. ''You just don't understand it. You're too old,'' I tell him.

I am hiking with Waiki from Florence to Siena. We spend the night in peasant houses, make love in the wide, old, creaky beds, make love in an olive grove, in a meadow behind a church, beneath pine trees on a knoll. We often walk along with our arms around each other. People give us grapes, and one time in a store someone gives us money. We accept it, thrilled by this new experience, this taste of an entirely different way of life. We are both stagestruck, and now we have succeeded in playing at least one role convincingly. In the next village we will give the money away, but until we get there it belongs to us. We continue on our way, singing. Then I see the old woman. She is seated on a stone in a vineyard, her head supported on her arthritic hand, her hair hidden under a kerchief. Everything about her looks weary: her stooped back, her grayish skin, her suspicious beady eyes. I stop and look at her, filled with pity and disgust. Suddenly I am overcome by the conviction that it is I who am sitting there, burned out, at a dead end. Tears stream down my face, I stumble a few steps forward, but when I turn around she has vanished. "What's wrong?" Waiki asks as he waits for me to catch up.

"In eight years we'll be thirty, Waiki. Then no one will give us money."

"No, probably not."

"Listen, do you know what that means, thirty? Only eight years from now! Is that even conceivable?"

"I guess it has to be."

"Eight years—that's a stretch of time you can get a sense of. Eight years ago we were fourteen, almost grown up."

"But only almost. Fourteen is a good age, right on the border line. That's when you should stop getting any older. After that, the difference between twenty and thirty is hardly worth mentioning."

"Oh, yes it is, Waiki, it's quite a difference. Now we are young, and in eight years we won't be. Will you even love me eight years from now?"

"I don't know. You can never tell about a thing like that ahead of time." He is offering no reassurance, only making my panic worse. Is a woman of thirty still desirable? When does all that stop? He does not know that I have just seen an apparition of my own old age and death. "It's quite likely I'll still love you when you're thirty." He sounds testy. I can expect no comfort from him. Thirty is old. At thirty one is lost to the world.

After that Italian journey we have thirteen more years together. During the first five of those years our playfulness more and more gives way to sobriety; Nazism is taking on an increasingly menacing aspect, overshadowing our professional studies. No plans can be made with any confidence. We realize that our lives are at stake, yet we draw no conclusions. Then comes the day of horror, January 30, 1933, followed by eight years of decline, during which we lose almost everything we called our own: our country, our language, our security, and finally our very identity.

At the entrance to every German town a sign is posted: JEWS ENTER AT THEIR OWN RISK. At first people make fun of it, for where in the world do you not enter at your own risk? Then a slight burning sensation develops, as if you had scratched yourself on a thorn, and finally the tip is deeply embedded in your flesh and throbs incessantly. A discreet invitation to a pogrom: it is open season on us. We are no longer what we were until only recently. At least not in the eyes of the others. But you cannot undergo a change in the eyes of others without your own sense of self changing as well.

After the war I often dream about Hitler. I meet him in various places, in his study, at the movies, atop a mountain, in the desert. I always try to strike up a conversation with him, to reach him with words. I never succeed.

My relationship to Judaism, lukewarm and lax, without clear contours. At home you never ask where a person comes from or what he is. You belong to the Jewish community but do not go to the synagogue. I submit to religious instruction as a necessary evil. Learn Hebrew prayers by rote; they do not cast light on any of the questions that preoccupy me. The holidays we celebrate are Christmas and Easter, not Hanukkah and Passover. In the early twenties I am forced to confront the growing anti-Semitism. My hurt feelings, my desire to feel I am part of something impel me to become a Zionist. I remain one for a few months, at the age when a person is searching for a place in the world without finding one. I very quickly realize that this is not for me. From then on I cling to the idea that it enriches a person to have two sets of roots. My two favorite landscapes: Bavaria and the Mediterranean. Access to both the splendor of European culture, at that time still untarnished and seemingly indestructible, and the knowledge of suffering born of eternal persecution. The triumphant rationality of the Enlightenment and the transcendent magical formula for the sole, invisible, omnipotent God, *adonai echod*. And yet, in spite of everything, I feel closer to Antigone than to Ruth.

Waiki laughs. And I laugh with him. We often laugh in those years of terror, and love each other and are more magnificently happy than would have been possible in normal times.

Emigration is not merely falling out of one's own social class into a lower one; emigration is plummeting into a bottomless chasm.

After that I never want to own more than I can carry with me in two suitcases. Yet I allow myself to be seduced by the consumer society, acquire a house, an apartment, an automobile.

In a photograph the Bavarian resistance heroine Sophie Scholl looks like Joan of Arc in the silent film by Dreyer. Reserved, pensive, decisive, her head slightly bowed, revealing the nape of her neck, left bare by her short-cropped hair. One cannot look at that vulnerable young neck without thinking of the guillotine that will sever it. That picture torments me, although all it shows is a beautiful young person.

The analogy between Sophie and Antigone is sound. Both of them people who go to the limit. Who give completely of themselves. Who care not for success but for obeying their own sense of necessity. Not comfortable to have around. Difficult. People who force us to think. Who prod our awareness.

But perhaps Antigone really wants nothing but to bury her brother. That union, always sought, never achieved, now consummated with a handful of earth.

Germany, my *terra firma*, which I must leave. France, Italy, England, Switzerland, America, Holland. The roulette wheel turns. I am the little ball that is sent hurtling around. In which slot will I come to rest?

Is loss of identity really such a misfortune? Would it have been better to remain a German Jew in Munich all my life? As an emigrée I experience things of which I knew nothing in my old identity: I have no rights, am cast out, a Jew among Jews. The slightest misstep can mean the end. Antigone is my companion. The girl who sets forth with her blind father and leads him through the mountains to the sea. Who sits in the shadow of the great olive tree mending nets, listening to the pounding of the surf, the mewing of the gulls as they plummet and soar, who comes to understand that the gods give man not a shred of help. What he makes of himself is entirely up to him.

History does us the favor of calling our own form of terrorism resistance. Since there is a reluctance to put Jews on the front lines, I am set to work forging identity papers and rubber stamps, but I would rather go along when bridges are to be dynamited and bombs planted. Indifferent to the fact that people will die as a result. Violence is necessary because the State has become a mass murderer.

As I sit there, gazing at Marlene, I feel a sudden nostalgia for the underground. The situation is similar, except that now I am alone, whereas in those days, in spite of being persecuted, we formed a community in which we could rely on one another. We did not inquire into a person's ideological persuasion; that was not important. What mattered was to save lives. Each of us was putting his life in jeopardy at every moment. "I couldn't say anything—it was too risky" was a sentiment I never heard until after the war, in Germany.

We discussed methods of resistance. Had differing viewpoints, without feeling any less close to one another. Each could think as he liked. The goal—a realistic, not a Utopian one—was never in doubt: freedom.

Nothing remains of that spirit. Suspicion, distrust, rivalry, enmity wherever you turn. Right now I could use someone to help me get through this Marlene episode. By myself I am no longer equal to the challenge. I have withdrawn to my old folks' refuge, and my passive curiosity about everything taking place around me refuses to be transformed into activity. I am a spectator, not a participant.

I would like to shake Marlene awake and tell her: Get up and get out of here. I am a tired old woman. I don't care what happens to you. Even though you girls have not told me anything, I know you are a terrorist's moll. I reject violence and those who support violence. I reject your belief that there can be a paradise on earth, and I certainly reject your hellish ways of bringing about this paradise. You are playing war games, meaningless, sickening games. And I want peace.

But I cannot say it. My wound prevents me. Marlene needs help, and so I help her. Without inquiring into her ideology.

15

Cautiously I get up from the bed, quietly take Friedel's manuscript about the liquidation of the Piotrkow ghetto from the bedside table, turn on the reading lamp, and sit down in the little leather chair. I read the report once more, although I know it almost by heart.

Petrikau 7/26/43

Very early in the morning—I am already up and prepared for the instruction I am scheduled to give the men—the order comes: "Entire company assemble." The sergeant major stands there before the troops and says with a smile that is half-embarrassed, half-sly: "I need thirty men for a special assignment." He orders various men to fall out to the left, then says, "The two noncoms, too." So I am part of the group for the "special assignment."

"The thirty men are to receive thirty rounds of ammunition from the arms room." The men are dismissed, and the sergeant turns to H.—I am standing next to him—and says, "You lead the men to the ghetto and relieve the Luftwaffe patrol there. Departure as soon as possible. You'll be relieved at 1:00 o'clock." Cursing, we go to pick up our ammunition.

We march through the town. On one side of me is T., a morose, embittered fellow who would like nothing better than to shoot down every young male Pole in sight. On the other side of me is H., good old H.

We enter the old section of the town, pass the destroyed synagogue, whose ceiling has remained intact and glows in vibrant ultramarine, with graceful white plaster ornamentation and Hebrew inscriptions. To our right a large, unattractive square, thronged with people. We see both police and military personnel. We cross the square toward a higher-ranking police officer. A Luftwaffe staff sergeant comes forward to meet us, urging us to hurry; they expected us to be here long ago. We march around the barbed-wire fence that encloses the ghetto and relieve the Luftwaffe patrols. The sergeant says our assignment is to cordon off the ghetto, and if anyone tries to get out we should shoot on sight.

Our patrol takes us first along the river, which looks shallow and sluggish. Then through the narrow streets of the old town, to one side the ghetto, to the other side abandoned, dilapidated houses. Everywhere it is as silent as the grave, and a cold, musty smell wafts toward us. Inside the ghetto most of the houses are also vacant. You can tell by the paper curtains which ones are inhabited.

We complete our rounds and find ourselves back at the square, where men are lined up in an open-square formation: Jews. The women inside the ghetto are crowded up against the barbed wire. It is amazing how calm the situation is, considering that thousands of people are present. Names are being called out by a Jew who is reading them in a businesslike manner from a list; at each name a man steps forward. The space around the men is largely empty, but the sides of the square are a wall of human beings. Police are posted on the open side of the formation. Behind them is the command post.

The command post is a precinct house of the Polish police, but SS men, police, and military personnel come and go there. A dingy, whitewashed room, with flies everywhere. Flies clinging to the walls and ceiling in black blotches. Through an open door one can see into the next room, where there is a varnished wardrobe with a cracked mirror mounted on one door. On a table lies a loaf of white bread from which someone has broken off a chunk. The bread is grayish black with flies. I am in no mood to join the Polish policemen sitting around, so I lean against the stove. A very smartly dressed civilian enters. He holds up his hands and asks whether he may wash up here. I am surprised that a civilian would venture in for such a trivial purpose. In the meantime another man enters, wearing a leather coat. He too has his hands in the air, and in an Austrian accent he tells the other man to come upstairs where there is a sink. As the man turns to follow him, I notice that his hands are bloody. I ask H. who these men are. "Isn't it obvious?" he growls reluctantly. "Gestapo."

Through the window of the police station I can see a large yellow sign with black lettering that says JEWISH FORCED LABOR CAMP. It is posted by the entrance to the ghetto, where the women are thronging. Most of them are well dressed. There are many kerchiefs, in every possible color, many attractive hairdos, and some of the girls are strikingly good-looking.

The women are all staring wide-eyed in one direction, as if bewitched. They are not chattering, just watching, pressing up to the fence. A police captain, a small lean man with olive skin, strikes the woman closest to the wire with his whip and summons the Jewish civil police, who click their heels when addressed. They pick up the barricades festooned with barbed wire and push them against the women, who slowly retreat, without uttering a sound. Being forced to move back seems to be merely an unpleasant interruption in their intent staring. I go outside but cannot determine what the women are staring at. The situation remains as before: groups are being put together. If a Jew wants to join a particular group, he is shouted at and driven back with blows and kicks. All this is taking place matter-of-factly, almost in slow motion. I feel as though this square with the ugly grayish-whitish buildings and the grayish-whitish sky above were cut off from the rest of the world. Yet pedestrians pass by, horse-drawn wagons clatter along the street, and the Polish police are sent out time and again to break up the crowds of curious onlookers.

As I turn around, I glimpse something directly behind the barbed wire, at the street corner nearest the throng of women: in the gutter the soles of a pair of women's shoes and two thin legs in gray stockings are visible. I know in a flash: The woman these legs belong to is dead. I move closer. A scrawny little woman is lying there, her face to the ground. Her threadbare coat is stained with blood at the level of the shoulder blades. Her dress has hitched up, and a patch of yellowish thigh shows. In her hand is a colorful shopping bag. No one looks in that direction or pays any attention to her, neither the Jewish women standing and waiting nor the policemen, who have to pass very close by her. When I look up, an SS man is standing beside me, a huge fellow with a deep tan. I ask him why the woman was shot. He looks down at me with his head cocked on one side, then stares straight ahead and snorts scornfully. I must have asked a very stupid question.

The young man mumbles so badly that I have to ask him to repeat it several times before I grasp what he is saying. But this much I get out of him: The Jews have dug two escape tunnels into the old town, which has been evacuated. In addition, a cellar converted into a bunker has been found, with seventeen pistols and a few homemade grenades in it. The Jews who fired from this cellar have been shot. That is why the ghetto is being cleared out.

"And what will happen to the Jews?"

"They will be taken away to work for the HASAG."

"What's the HASAG?"

"A large firm, with several factories here."

The sound of a policeman angrily swearing makes me look in his direction. With cuffs and blows he is driving a Jew up onto a green truck that is already packed like a sardine can. "What will happen with the men on the truck?" I ask the SS man.

"They're going to Palestine." As if to reassure me, he adds, "They don't know that. They think they are being taken to the HASAG."

I look at the faces of the men on the truck. They show no emotion, no expression. A policeman jumps onto the truck, takes up a position in the rear, pulls a long loaf of white bread out of one Jew's pocket, and as the truck begins to move tosses it to another policeman, while the Jew stares numbly after his bread. I see the accompanying vehicle start up. Rests for the submachine guns are mounted up front, and the policemen stand behind them in firing position as they speed along behind the truck.

I go back into the command post. H. is sitting there, looking straight ahead. The Gestapo agents are at the table, chatting and cleaning the blood off their revolvers with an old towel. They are discussing one of their fellow agents: "Have you ever seen him do an interrogation?" asks the one in the Tyrolean hat, and then continues, "He has three guys in front of him.

'Were you present when it happened?' he asks the first one, and when he says, 'No'—bang, bang! He asks the second guy, and he doesn't answer—bang, bang! He asks the third, and even before he can say anything—bang, bang.''

This method of interrogation amuses all his listeners, and in fact, the faces of the German and Polish policemen sitting around convey the impression that the whole thing is just fun and games to them. The SS man tells jokes and the Polish policemen struggle to follow his German. A heavyset police lieutenant with short-cropped white hair and round brown eyes enters, and the policemen snap to attention. He gestures to them to be seated. He mops his brow and joins the circle. ''I go to a hotel with a friend, have a good meal and a few drinks, and finally the waiter brings the check: fifty zlotys—'' At that moment shots ring out outside, several in quick succession. I rush out, and see a few policemen hurrying past the old woman in the gutter and entering a building. A moment later more shots are heard. I think I should alert the patrol, that something should be done. Nothing happens. After a while I go back into the police station, where the SS man is still telling his joke about the fifty zlotys. In the course of the day many more shots were fired inside the ghetto, and no one inquired what was going on.

Someone brings the police lieutenant a large, battered, reddish brown suitcase. He opens it, takes out some old blue rags, which he tosses under the table, then sends the suitcase out to the captain. I am curious to know what the suitcase is for. When I step outside, the green truck is back, already jammed with Jews again. Only now do I realize what the women have been staring at with such fascination: the truck. To the rear of the truck stands a Jew who takes his greasy yarmulke from his bald head and again and again passes his trembling hands over his face, his eyes glazed with terror. When the lieutenant approaches, he bends far forward, hands outstretched, and in a pleading, tearful voice repeats over and over, "I'm not to blame, Lieutenant, sir!" A Jew standing next to him also stretches out his arms and calls, "Lieutenant, sir! Lieutenant, sir!" The other men on the truck keep silent. One of them has his head bowed and his hands crossed on his chest; perhaps he is praying. These men do not believe they are being taken to the HASAG. The truck drives off, and the eyes of the Jew who kept calling out "Lieutenant, sir!" grow unnaturally large. At that moment one man on the truck pulls himself up to his full height, so that he appears taller than all the rest, raises his clenched fist, and shouts, "Red Front!" Two other fists wave in the air. I look over toward the women; they are all standing there staring, those in front pushed against the barbed wire, silent, unmoving; only a few wave after the truck, which disappears from view at the other end of the square, behind it the police vehicle. No one calls after the men, no one sobs, everything remains as before.

Now the women watch the men file past the open suitcase. All money and valuables must be deposited in it. That takes a long time. Then the men are lined up in rows, five abreast, and at long last the procession gets under way—to the HASAG. As he passes, one Jew tips his hat to the SS man standing outside the command post, calls out something to him, and the SS man replies cheerily. Apparently the police and the SS man know many of the Jews by name, are familiar with their circumstances—"There goes my old pal the director," "Look, that's my boy Rosenbaum," etc.

When the square is empty, you can see that it is littered with keys and small change. Things they will not be needing. T., who is on guard duty, keeps a sharp eye out and occasionally bends to pick up something. H. goes to him and forbids him to take anything, lest he harm the reputation of the Wehrmacht. No sooner is H. back than we see T. bending down again.

Now one of the barricades wound with barbed wire is shoved to one side, forming a narrow passageway through which the women are let out one at a time. A young rosy-cheeked policeman stands by the open suitcase and calls out again and again: "Money, jewelry, rings, earrings—everything in here!" He calls after those who have already surrendered their valuables, "We'll search everybody, and you'll have cause to regret it if we find anything on you!" One girl twists and twists at her ring and finally says, "It won't come off." "Oh, so it won't come off, will it," the policeman says, and grabs her wrist. She holds perfectly still, utters a brief cry, then laughs, as though someone had played too rough in a game; the ring tumbles into the suitcase. The women rummage through their pocketbooks and bundles, struggle with earrings. More and more money falls into the suitcase. A banknote flutters out of a woman's hand and lands next to the suitcase, but she picks it up and tosses it in. The women are lined up in rows, five abreast, at the upper end of the square.

The little four-seater I noticed before returns, and the two Gestapo agents climb out, holding their machine guns. By now I can predict just what will happen. First the four-seater returns, then the police vehicle, finally the green truck, empty. The SS man asks the one in the Tyrolean hat, "Well, how was it?" He replies with a laugh, "They're all hard at work at the HASAG by now." The bystanders laugh knowingly.

I see a little boy of about five, wearing a coat that is much too long for him, running along the deserted street toward the ghetto. I do not know why the boy is running. A policeman points out the boy to one of the Jewish civil policemen. The policeman chases him, and the boy runs even faster—yet no matter how comical this game of catch looks, no one laughs. The civil policeman catches the boy and carries him back. The boy does not stir, merely gazes around with wide gray eyes. At this moment I see women and girls, children either in their arms or holding their hands, being driven across the street. Two old women and an elderly man with thick white eyebrows are among them—I simply had not noticed any of them before this. They are led into a large, windowless shed next to the command post, which probably once served as a garage. From the group comes a general whimpering, a thin whine, which grows louder as they enter the shed and can still be heard, though muffled, after a policeman has secured the door with a padlock.

At that moment a little girl of perhaps seven approaches from the open side of the square, where the Polish bystanders keep gathering. She is all by herself, and I do not understand why she should be coming from this direction, for nowhere do I see anyone who might have ordered her to do so. She calmly goes up to the locked door, the policeman opens it, she goes inside.

The police vehicle returns. The men are agitated, laughing nervously and cursing. One of them, standing next to me, takes off his helmet and mops his brow. He has a narrow, pleasant-looking face. "No, sir," he says. "I've seen a lot, but never anything like this!"

"What happened?"

"When the Jews noticed we were headed for the cemetery, they threw money out of the truck. Like fools, we hadn't taken the goods away from this batch. It was raining five-hundred-zloty bills, watches, and rings, and the Polacks ran along behind and grabbed what they could. Suddenly the tailgate flew open—the Jews must have unfastened it—and they came pouring out of the truck. We opened fire immediately; I yelled to the others to aim high so they wouldn't hit the driver and the guard up front in the truck. The driver had no idea what was going on. He stepped on the gas and tore off. We raced along behind, firing constantly, bumping like crazy over the bodies lying in the road, so we thought we might tip over any moment. We got to the cemetery with a total of five men still alive—and you can bet they didn't stay that way very long."

The patrolman who was with the police escort joins the group and laughs at the tale. "But," says the policeman who is telling it, "we got all of them." A Luftwaffe sergeant joins us; he says he knocked off a few of the Jews who had jumped off the truck and tried to escape into a wheat field. "Those were the ones who shouted, 'Long live Moscow!' as they drove off." (I had not heard any such thing.) And by way of explanation he tells me, "When you're dealing with criminals like that, you can't help getting caught up in your job." This was the same staff sergeant who an hour earlier had said, "This kind of thing's not for me; I'm a soldier, not a hangman. That's what our commander says, too. He always puts up a devil of a fuss when he's told to send us on an assignment like this." He had even added with disgust that that morning in the command post he had heard a policeman ask his superior whether he wanted coffee, whereupon the superior had answered, "What do I need coffee for? I want blood—blood!"

Midday is already long past, and I am feeling faint. I sit down in the command post. Outside I hear someone shout, "A chair! Bring a chair!" A policeman hurries inside and fetches a chair. I go outside, and the green truck is back. A commotion around it. Already on the truck are a couple of adults, a few young women, toward the front an old woman in a red-and-black checked dress. A tall, thin policeman is shouting as he directs the proceedings. His helmet must be too small for him, for it perches ridiculously on the top of his head. With a brown oak cane he strikes the old man with a turned-up coat collar who is trying in vain to get onto the high-bodied truck. Now I understand what the chair was needed for. The old man scrambles up. He is followed by an old woman. The policeman shoves her so hard she falls face forward into the truck. Then the policeman bends down—I cannot see too clearly because of the crowd in front of me—and picks up something that he tosses onto the truck. It is a child. It bounces off the adults who are standing too close to the edge of the truck and tumbles down. In a rage the policeman grabs his cane and beats the adults to make them back up. Then he bends down again, and one bundle after another goes flying onto the truck. When I get a clear view for a moment, I can see a little girl holding out her arms to the policeman as she realizes he is about to pick her up. From behind the skirt of a woman on the truck the inquisitive black eyes of a little boy keep peeping out. Then a white bundle flies up, and the women hold out their arms to catch it. It is a child of about one in a

161

little white coat and cap. For seconds it appears to hover in the air, wearing a perfectly calm, serious expression, while all the available light on this gray day seems concentrated on this startlingly white spot. Then the child disappears into the interior of the truck, a few more are pitched up, and the tailgate is banged shut.

To the rear of the truck stands a young woman with a strong, vigorous face. She shouts and curses in Polish, and in between she exclaims over and over again. "Oh! Oh!" She is trying desperately to explain something to the policemen, finally shouting in pidgin German, "Me twenty-three years old, me no child!" I do not know what she wants to say. Was she put on the truck by mistake, is she not the mother of any of the children? Her face is beet red. "Oh! Oh!" she cries.

I look toward the higher end of the sloping square. Hundreds of women are waiting there, their backs to the truck. Apparently they have been ordered to turn away. The light-colored dresses and coats of the women form a whitish wall. Many of them peek furtively over their shoulders at the truck. Then the truck starts up with a jerk and lumbers off, the policemen jump into their vehicle, which is directly behind it, and set their submachine guns in the rests. The trip to the Jewish cemetery takes about twenty minutes.

It is all happening so matter-of-factly, almost as if it were perfectly natural. Not one of the mothers screamed to the heavens, there was no flailing about, no raving, no raging. Everything takes its course. The atmosphere is leaden. The women in the square face front again.

H. sends me off to check on the patrols. I pass very close to the women. I particularly notice one in the front row; she is wearing a white lab coat and cap, in all likelihood a nurse. She stands there very straight, holding a bundle. As I go by, two black eyes gaze at me without seeing me, gentle, earnest, full of dreadful suspense. Actually, all the women have the same look in their eyes. When shots ring out, a soft moan goes through their ranks. No tears are to be seen, and for a moment I think: All these women and girls are standing here dreaming.

Schm. comes toward me along the cobbled alley, his gun resting on his forearm in firing position. Ahead of him walks a stocky young man. He has no shirt on, just some old rags wrapped around him. Schm. reports: ''The Security Service was evacuating the bridge behind the ghetto; this man broke into a run, and a Ukrainian aimed at him, but I stopped him from firing.'' I order Schm. to turn the man over to the police. Schm. asks me to come along. I escort him to the command post.

The little olive-skinned captain is standing in front of the command post with policemen clustering around him. Schm. reports to him, points out the man, the captain thanks him and gestures with his head to one of the policemen. The policeman tells the prisoner, ''Come on, you're going with me,'' and takes him to the big shed where the women and children were taken earlier. The door has scarcely closed behind them when two shots are fired inside.

The women are told to wheel to the left and march off—to the HASAG.

An older policeman is standing next to me. He has a large black dog on a leash and a pipe in his mouth. He is the epitome of the decent public servant grown gray in office. I ask him, ''Now that the Jews have all been taken away, won't this assignment be over soon?'' He removes his pipe from his mouth and says, ''There are still some sick ones who have to be put out of their misery.'' He makes this remark in an unnecessarily loud voice, apparently very pleased with his formulation, and the other policemen laugh approvingly.

The police vehicle takes me and half of the guard detail to lunch. In the meantime the weather has cleared up. Deep blue sky, sunshine, a gentle summer breeze. It is amazing how quickly and smoothly the large vehicle rides.

We arrive back at the square. I notice that the Gestapo agents have changed their clothes. Now they have on light-colored, elegant jackets and dark trousers. One of the men is wearing a blue silk shirt that zips down the front. They are cradling their submachine guns in their hands, praising the weapon: ''You can't beat a submachine gun. When I fired this baby a while back, the man's head flew right off his shoulders.'' ''Yes,'' the other one says, ''the bursts of fire have a terrific punch to them.''

Two older policemen are sitting out in front of the command post. They have taken off their helmets and are basking in the sun. I am surprised they are allowed to relax this way while on duty. They say the lieutenant gave them permission. One of them, a weary-looking man with white hair, asks me whether we soldiers all fold our pants around to the front inside our boots, and whether we are permitted to have our ties show more than a whisker above the collar. I cannot help laughing at the way the two are teasing me. I ask them whether they got off plenty of shots here while I was at lunch. ''No, not us!'' The other man, lean and bald with good-natured russet-brown eyes, says, ''I hate being part of this. But there's not a thing you can say. At least I've never taken part in an execution. And I wouldn't, either.''

''But what if you were ordered to?''

"I would ask the captain to let me off."

"Do you think he would?"

"Yes, I mean, I don't know—but I wouldn't do it," he insists, "I couldn't make myself. We had a patrolman a while back who was ordered to shoot the children of the Jewish intellectuals. There were some little darlings among them, believe me. For a week after that he didn't show up for work, did nothing but drink. He said he couldn't help thinking of his own children the whole time. We were all afraid something would happen to him. But the captain put him on furlough for two weeks, sent him back to Germany to his family."

The little four-seater is parked right in front of us on the street. It is empty. A Gestapo agent appears with a man in handcuffs, shoves him into the car, and goes away again. The man's skin is so dark he looks like a Hungarian Gypsy. He sits there alone in the car, leaning back against the cushions. He does not look as if he had sat in a car very often. His eyes too have that gentle, strained look. What does it express— numbness, acceptance, horror? A driver and two Gestapo men come and get into the car. One of them kicks the prisoner in the calf to make him move over; on each side of him sits an agent with a submachine gun. After a short interval the four-seater returns. One of the policemen asks. "Hey, where did you take him so fast?"

"He's gone, that's all you need to know."

The police captain comes up to me and asks whether I have eaten already. "Yes, Captain, sir."

"You sure? Don't be shy, now." What a pleasant, resonant bass voice the little man has. "You can have them give you something inside."

"Thank you, Captain, sir, I've eaten."

He asks whether his own men have eaten, asks

each one of them, asks about those who are not present, then wants to know whether they were also all given schnapps. Yes, they were. He asks the lieutenant whether he couldn't dole out another ration. The lieutenant replies with a smile that he is saving some for the execution squad. The captain nods.

The Luftwaffe sergeant appears again and tells me he ate here in the ghetto a few days ago. "In the ghetto? Does it have a restaurant for Germans?"

"At first I thought my buddies were just pulling my leg, but then I went along one time. And let me tell you, I've never eaten so well anywhere else in Poland. A steak so tender it melted on your tongue. And chicken with rice, and wine."

"Where did you get it?"

"Oh, the Jewish civil policemen bring it to you."

"But how could you let yourselves be fed by Jews?"

"I'm telling you, I haven't had such a good meal in ages! And you should have seen what the policemen polished off in there—Lord preserve us!"

A Gestapo agent appears behind the barbed wire with a man in blue cotton work clothes. He calls out to us, "Look, I've got one of the moles." Presumably he means one of the men who helped dig the tunnel. The man has a blue jacket over his arm, and he too looks at us out of calm black eyes. You might think he was just on his way home from work if the Gestapo agent were not standing beside him with his submachine gun, holding him by the shirt with two fingers, the way you would hold on to a child. They pass close by the old woman who is still lying in the gutter and go through the gateway of a large, plain, gray building on the left. For some reason one of the walls along the driveway is whitewashed, but the whitewash has faded in places. The men have barely disappeared when another shot is heard.

A truck drives up. It is not the familiar green one but another, gray and low-slung. Girls and women with children, all noticeably well dressed, come out of the ghetto with the Jewish civil policemen and hastily toss bundles, large sacks, and all sorts of housewares onto the truck. The things pile up, and some of them fall off. The captain notices this, goes over to the women and says, "There's no rush. Take the stuff out and load it properly so that everything fits in."

They obey. My attention is caught by two ladies—their dress and bearing make this word come to mind. Both of them are very slim, both dressed in black. One of them is carrying a little child in light-colored clothes. She reminds me somewhat of Eleonora Duse. "What will be done with those people?" I ask the SS man. "Those are the families of the civil policemen. They come last. But they all have their turn."

"Why all of them? Even those who were just taken to the HASAG?"

"Sure. They'll stay only until the HASAG has enough Poles."

I still have trouble with his mumbling. "Did you say all of them?" I ask.

"All of them."

A guard brings a man with a mass of blond curls. His face is bloody, beaten beyond recognition. I do not know how the man can still walk or grasp the orders he is given. He is sent to the entrance to the ghetto, where a civil policeman is supposed to keep an eye on him.

There is a great rumbling on the cobblestones, and three large horse-drawn carts lumber up. The carts have no sides, only a few boards nailed across the front and the back. Huge trays on wheels. The police barricades wound with barbed wire are moved away from the entrance, and the teams thunder into the ghetto. From the gateway to the gray building, Jewish civil policemen carry out something on an empty burlap bag and take it to the first cart—all I can see is a bloody hand. Then they go back into the entryway. The old policeman with the black dog says to the captain, ''While they're at it, they should take away that old biddy there who decided to fall down in such an awkward place.'' He has a comical way of expressing himself. The captain calls to the civil policemen, who click their heels and leap into action. They haul the old woman away by her hands and feet.

From the entrance to the ghetto I see four men lined up diagonally across the street. Three of them have spades in their hands. They stand there perfectly quietly, waiting for something. I cannot see anyone supervising them. The fourth is the man with the mass of blond curls and the bloodied face. Finally a Jewish civil policeman comes along, hands the curly-head a spade, and orders the four to proceed ahead of him. As they go into the entryway of the gray building, the significance of the spades becomes clear to me. The three carts, two of them empty, drive in after the men.

I walk along the perimeter of the ghetto enclosure. I can look into the dirty courtyard behind the building, through whose gateway the carts just passed. The carts are drawn up side by side in the courtyard, waiting.

I continue to where the fence ends. There I see a low stone building, painted white, with flower boxes at the windows. I hear firm steps crunching behind me and turn around: inside the fence the tall policeman with the comical little helmet and the cane is approaching, behind him four Jewish civil policemen carrying axes and cleavers. The policeman reaches the door of the stone building, and presses the latch. Locked. He rings the bell next to the door. It resounds shrilly. The policeman keeps his finger on the bell. Finally the door opens, and a rotund little nurse appears. She stares in panic at the policeman, who asks, "Do you have any stretchers?" She does not answer. The policeman turns to the civil policeman: "Ask the woman whether she has any stretchers." Then he pushes his way into the building, the policemen behind him, and the door closes.

I walk around the building, which occupies a corner of the ghetto. I see the narrow side of it, then a high plank fence. A few guards are standing huddled in a group. I order them back to their posts. V. says, "All the patients are supposed to be killed." B., who looks so serious and reserved and is a man of few words, says, "That's how it should be, because if they're going to die anyway, what's the point of going on treating them?" V.: "Well, in that case there would be no point in treating you, since you're going to die too someday!" N., a lazy fellow who is forever grousing and hates being a soldier: "You asshole! Sometimes you come up with some really shitty ideas!"

A policeman appears in the garden behind the plank fence and begins to break out slats from the smaller fence that separates the hospital grounds from the interior of the ghetto. A voice calls out to him, "Why are you doing that? It's totally superfluous!" "No," the policeman replies, and continues smashing the slats, "we can take them right through this way and needn't bring them across the street first." "Oh, if you like," the voice answers. I continue on my way.

The tall plank fence that blocks the view into the

ghetto continues only a short distance, then comes a low fence, over which one can easily see into a gloomy courtyard, with patches of high grass in the shadow of scattered bushes. The rear of the courtyard is formed by the high, windowless gray wall of a building, in front of it a one-story block in grayish brown stone. It is uninhabited, without windows or doors. About ten policemen are standing silently around the neglected courtyard. To the right is the gap in the fence that leads to the hospital grounds. Where are they going to take the patients? I wonder.

At one spot in the fence where the vertical slats have been broken out, a girl climbs through, followed by a fat blond policeman. The black-haired girl looks firm and healthy, not at all like a hospital patient. I might take her for a country girl from southern Germany. She is wearing a dressing gown, black with pink flowers. "Go along now," the policeman says, and points toward the farther reaches of the courtyard. I notice that he uses the formal mode of address. The girl goes on ahead of him, exclaiming in an agitated, tearful voice, "But I want to go to HASAG!" And she turns around to him—now I can see her from the front—and exclaims again, "I want to go to HASAG!" After the word HASAG she utters a little cry and raises her hands. She sees the mouth of a revolver pointing at her; the policeman is standing two meters away and shoots her in the chest. She falls, as if struck by lightning. The policeman steps forward and fires a few more shots into her. I cannot see the scene clearly because the tall grass hides her.

At that moment another girl is already coming through the gap in the fence, in a sky-blue bathrobe. She is flaxen blond, and I see a profile with a delicate pale pink complexion, the sun shimmering through the soft down on her cheeks. The policeman with the cane appears next to her and says, "Come along now, nothing's going to happen to you!"

She advances a few steps into the courtyard. The policemen cannot shoot because the other policeman is still in the line of fire. The girl notices the first girl lying there, hesitates, and for a moment there is utter silence. Then—the policeman with the cane has stepped aside in the meantime—shots ring out. The girl keels over as if invisible hands were pulling her. Her arms make no attempt to break the fall. Her bathrobe gets twisted, and there is a glimpse of her naked buttocks. A policeman steps up close to her. I continue on my way. Another shot is fired. Shortly thereafter more shots. I myself have often fired a weapon and have spent many hours on the shooting stand supervising the range, but I never knew shots to be so loud, so ear-splitting.

I return to the fence. Three meters away from me lies a tall, slender, black-haired girl on her stomach, one side of her face turned toward me. A policeman is bending over her. He shoots three times in rapid succession into her head. The head jerks up a bit each time, but the face remains perfectly tranquil, like that of someone brushing away a fly as she sleeps. Blood oozes out of her hair as if someone were wringing out a sponge filled with a light, oily liquid. Then a cascade of blood suddenly bursts from her nose. To think that so much blood can spurt out of the nostrils at once.

I continue on again. Behind the fence I hear a voice calling out, "Have the dames been taken care of?" "No," comes the answer, "there are two left."

"Bring them out!"

After a while I hear the same voice again, "Come on, honey, lie down now!" A pause. Then the same voice shouts hoarsely, "I said *lie down!*" A shot—and another shot. In the Polish house closest to the ghetto, people are crowded in the doorways. I see a woman who is leaning against a man start at every shot and press her hand to her mouth.

I force myself to go back once more. One policeman calls out to another, "He's had four shots, and the pig is still grunting!" He pushes the man around with his boot, wants to shoot again, but the others restrain him. A waste of ammunition. A man in gray-and-purple striped pajamas comes into the courtyard. He walks very calmly, his head bent, as if he were lost in thought. A shot is fired. I go far up the river, passing my men at their posts. They make their reports to me.

When the shooting has stopped, I pass by again. The green grass is dotted with colorful little heaps. One man without a stitch of clothing on. The girl in sky blue is now lying oddly on her back, her open eyes staring into the heavens. Her limbs are snow-white, like a wax doll's. Near the fence lies the man in pajamas, his knees drawn up as if he had just curled up to go to sleep. How tranquil all the faces are, no grimaces, no sign of terror. Two skinny male legs, naked, stick up out of the bushes. Not a scream, not a curse, not a prayer was heard here. They all let themselves be led to the slaughter without outcry.

Now I hear policemen behind the gray building. One of them is scolding, "Get to work! Get to work! Let's have it over with! Move that shovel, you bastard!" I go along until I can see in through the entryway. I see a wall of earth and a shovelful of dirt being pitched into it. I cannot see those who are doing the shoveling. I sniff the air and wonder: What's that sweetish smell? Then I realize: blood.

When I return to the courtyard after a while, it is empty. Only pools of blood and slippers scattered around. In the middle is a green-embroidered pair with high heels.

As I pass the hospital, the doctor and two nurses in white coats are coming out. They run toward the entrance to the ghetto. A truck is there, loaded with Jewish men and women, who call out to the three that they should hurry. They scramble onto the truck. But it does not start up yet. I do not know what the truck is waiting for. I glance in at the window of the command post and see H. sitting there leafing through a magazine. He does not want to see or hear anything. I wonder whether this is the right way to behave. No, not for me.

The captain is sitting in his car, and I hear him say to the lieutenant, "Tell the doctor he's being resettled," and then he corrects himself: "No, resettled doesn't sound good, tell him he's being taken somewhere else." The lieutenant leaves. "Anton will be angry at me today," the captain says to the bystanders (Anton is apparently one of the Jewish civil policemen). "We assured him his family would be spared, and now we've done away with his father and mother. Of course it's hard for these people. But if you insist on having sentimental attachments, you can't handle the situation. If the Jews could have their way, they'd ship us all off to Siberia, and I can guarantee you only a fraction of us would survive the trip."

A pretty, plump girl holding a bundle comes running out of the ghetto. Her face is flushed with exertion. "Where did you come from?" the lieutenant asks.

"The infirmary."

"The infirmary? Get back!"

"But the captain said I could—" she pants. The

173

captain turns and gestures to the lieutenant, who lets the girl pass. She jumps onto the truck.

I notice a girl of about twelve on the truck. Her head barely shows above the sideboards, a narrow face with pale, yellowish skin and almond-shaped eyes. All the people on the truck are gentle to her, stroke her, speak encouragingly to her. She is perfectly calm. Speaks a clear, pure German in a somewhat weary voice. "What's the story with the girl?" the lieutenant asks in a kindly manner, going up close to the truck. A heavy woman with bleached hair sitting next to the girl says, "We all look out for her." I do not dare to ask where the girl's parents are. "Take her along to Katz," the lieutenant says. (I do not know what *Katz* refers to.) "Oh no, Lieutenant, sir, please let me take the child with me to the foundry," says the platinum blonde. "What could she do in the foundry?" the lieutenant asks, and turns to the girl directly: "Well, my child, where do you want to go?" She looks calmly at the lieutenant and says, "To Katz!" "Fine, my child," the lieutenant says, and instructs the driver accordingly. The platinum blonde makes a despairing gesture. After a while she says, "Lieutenant, sir, I left my coat in the ghetto." "I told all of you to take along your coats," the lieutenant scolds them good-naturedly. "Well, get down, but make it snappy!" The heavy woman does not have an easy time of it getting off the truck. The lieutenant holds out his hand to her: "Hop down, girl!" She lets herself tumble into his arms, laughing self-consciously. Other women begin to scramble over the sides of the truck. Helpful policemen reach up to catch them. The women run as fast as they can into the ghetto.

If you did not know what was going on here and saw this scene, you would think the truck was full of emigrants to whom the German police were being helpful and reassuring.

One policeman stands inside the fenced-off ghetto and calls out to another who is waiting by the truck: "Hey, didn't you just bump off three dames in there?"

"Sure I did, what of it?"

"Maybe you could do something about getting them out of there!"

A couple of civil policemen go into the shed where the women and children were taken earlier. I know why they are being sent in. They carry an uncovered corpse right past the truck. The women stare down numbly at it.

First one woman, then another comes back with her coat, and all of them have thrown together extra bundles. I am surprised that the men do not go to fetch their coats likewise, but they do not stir. A strikingly pale young man with long hair falling across his forehead leans back in the corner of the truck as if it were an easy chair.

A rack wagon comes clattering rapidly down the sloping street of the ghetto. Three women are lying in it, facedown. They wobble like gelatine. The lieutenant calls out to the Jew driving the wagon, each time giving him different orders. And each time the Jew obeys. One time he leaps with catlike agility onto the wagon and grabs the reins. Another time he jumps off and runs to the lieutenant. Finally the wagon rattles away, into the entryway to the large gray building.

I sit down in front of the command post. I have been hanging around here for almost twelve hours now. The truck has driven away. The large square is empty and silent. Occasionally a policeman or guard goes off to attend to something. Dusk is blurring the colors and contours of the square and the ghetto.

Still no shots to be heard? They must need a fairly large pit. Perhaps the ground there is hard and rocky. And probably the men with the shovels do not have much strength left for their task. I get up and pace back and forth across the square. I see H. stepping out in front of the command post. I do not feel in the mood to talk with him, or with anyone. Then a few muffled shots can be heard in the distance. After that, silence. A short while later shots again.

The captain, who has been gone in the meantime, drives up in his little open car and stops. There is something peaceful and contented about the way he leans back in his seat, his limbs relaxed after a hard day's work, and quietly converses with the others in the car. They are talking less loudly than before.

Very close to me is the lieutenant. He calls a patrolman over. I hear him say, "I have to report to the captain how many were done away with today. Toni and I took care of a hundred thirty between us, fifty at the commissary," and I cannot hear the rest. I only hear the patrolman exclaim, "And then there were the two from the bunker," to which the lieutenant replies impatiently, "Oh, never mind, we don't have to account for every single one!" He goes over to the car and delivers his report, which I cannot hear. Then comes the captain's deep voice; "Well, the men have certainly earned their schnapps!" He drives away. Immediately afterward, the three wagons rattle out of the ghetto—empty. The lieutenant sees me standing there and remarks, "Yes, getting rid of men is easy, you know, but women and children, that's shitwork. Well, good night!"

"Good night, Lieutenant, sir!"

The policemen cluster around. They are in a good mood, all talking at the same time. The one with the narrow face comes up to me and says, "Whew, that was a hot day! The worst part was at the cemetery with the women and children. What a scene they put on!''

"In what way?"

"I mean until we finally got the kids away from the women. But the old ones were quiet as lambs. They went and stood on the edge of the grave, got their kick in the butt, and then—pow! pow! We're going to go celebrate now. Heil Hitler!''

"Heil Hitler!'' The policemen get into their vehicle.

One patrolman is still there. He sits down on a chair and lights up a cigarette. It glows in the dark. A Jewish civil policeman comes up to him, clicks his heels and says, "Patrolman, sir, the civil police force is all out of cigarettes.'' The patrolman calls a Polish policeman and orders him to go somewhere with the Jew and buy cigarettes. The Jew thanks him.

The tall SS man comes over to us and tells us we may leave. We summon the men on patrol duty, form up ranks, and march off. N. tells me he saw them take an infant out of its mother's arms in the courtyard and shoot it, shooting the mother immediately after that. He will not be able to sleep for a few nights, he says. A few others chime in that they will not be able to sleep either. "That really shook me up,'' they say.

As we march back through the darkened streets of the old town and hear the sharp, rhythmic sound of our marching feet echoing back and forth, H. remarks, "Anyone seeing us here will think we've been slaughtering people left and right, and yet our hands are perfectly clean.'' Amazingly enough, it is T. who comments, "The others in the company will think we reek of blood.''

We turn into the brightly lit main thoroughfare, and I hear P. saying softly behind me, "Hey, shooting men and women, that's all right, if it has to be done. But innocent little children, that's where I draw the line." We march to our barracks. H. orders us to unload our guns and fall out.

I let the manuscript sink into my lap. Marlene is tossing restlessly, but she does not wake up.

I am weary to death, drained of hope. I hear shots, hear whimpering. The naked corpses are lying heaped up near the weathered tombstones. I bury my face in my hands.

16

Two people are standing in the room. They must have come in without ringing the bell. Christine and a tall, handsome young man. "This is Frank." She has never brought him to see me, never mentioned that he is good-looking. Perhaps she would laugh if I said anything about it: You really think so, Auntie? What difference does it make?

My initial alarm at their sudden appearance gives way to a profound sense of calm. Frank radiates tranquility. He has a round face like Antigone's shepherd. In Apulia I once stood in the middle of a herd of sheep that was being driven from a lower level up a steep bank to a higher plateau. There was a muffled thump; a ewe had thrown a lamb as she trotted along. The shepherd picked it up, slung it across his shoulders, carried it up the slope, and put it down next to its mother. A primeval gesture of helping. Frank leans over Marlene, takes her tenderly in his arms, and kisses her awake. "Time to get up, baby, we've found a great place for you. You can stay there as long as you like." She smiles, then her face puckers up, and it looks as though she is about to scream, but he holds her tightly, strokes her, is so much in control that her incipient hysteria is nipped in the bud.

I feel jealousy, real, foolish jealousy, but then I think smugly: How nice to be past the age of leaning one's head on a man's chest, now nice not to have the problem of coping or failing to cope with a sudden crush. Instead, one can enjoy the crush in peace.

Marlene is up now. Frank takes her by the arm, while Christine carries her bag. " 'Bye," says my strange guest. Not another word. Christine kisses me. "It was awfully decent of you." Frank nods to me, in a mixture of appreciation and condescension.

When they are gone, I want to go into the living room, but my legs are trembling, my knees buckle. I am as exhausted as if I had been on one of those big mountain climbs on which you are forced to turn back before reaching the peak. Patches of fog over the slopes. Your goal inaccessible. Cursing out loud, I undress and creep into the bed, still warm from her young body.

A condition somewhere between sleeping and waking. I feel hot, I feel cold. I have drawn up my legs and am lying there like an embryo. I want to go home, to be protected. Am everywhere and nowhere, am myself and others too. Ride a splendidly bridled steed over broad plans, sleep in a tent at the foot of the mountains with the dark prince, dissolve in tenderness, glide over the snow on skis, struggle through brambles, spread my arms and fly above the clouds through the deep blue sky. Smell the fragrance of the macchia and the creosote of the Schouwburg, hear music and cries and groans and sobs and thundering bells, see my parents lying together and making love in long white nightshirts, see young dogs romping and children burned by napalm, see the Death Steps with the prisoners in striped suits. I push them aside, run up the steps and back down, and cannot find Waiki, feel kisses on my skin and am beaten with a whip until I collapse.

I sit in a cave, trembling with the cold and damp, am hungry and thirsty, have to die, want to die, cannot die; dying is something you have to master. I am often amazed at how many people manage to die. In the end they are dead, have got it behind them, while I still have it before me. It would be nice to do it with a bit of style, "as a soldier stout and true," like Valentine in *Faust*, as one has lived, or believes one has lived.

She is sitting there on my bed, dressed in yellow. Light as a feather, beaming.

You are stealing my death from me. That is not fair—my death belongs to me and me alone. The poets who had so much to say about my life stopped there. When I was left alone in the dark cave, they withdrew. Let messengers report my suicide. Some of them had me stab myself with a dagger, others had me hang myself. All of them found it understandable that I should have cut short my life voluntarily, yet they were wrong about my reasons. I did it not in order to be dead sooner; the idea did not come to me until Haemon's slave had almost finished rolling aside the boulder at the mouth of the cave, when I saw light flooding in and realized I was supposed to be dragged back into the bonds of conventionality. As soon as I had returned to Thebes after Father's death, I had acceded to Haemon's urging and become engaged to him. I did not love him, for my heart was full of Polyneices, but there was an old, old familiarity; my mother and his father had been sister and brother, and we had played together from the time we were very young, he following me around everywhere like a puppy. He was so sweet, but a bit dull and dry, and he always swore he wanted to do everything for me, without understanding that I wanted no such thing. I wanted to stand with both feet on the ground and at the same time to fly off to uncharted higher regions. That was something I could do only with Polyneices. Now, after my brother's death, marriage was impossible for me, everything was impossible, life itself. So the only thing left was death. Up to this moment I had been willing to accept a slow death. Suffering is part of being human. Suffering is the province of my lover-god, of him who leads the starry light through the purple glow of night, who dies and is reborn. Draining the goblet to its depths, the sweet goblet of life, at whose bottom lurks horror, bitter as gall, yet still better than nothing.

My suicide was quickly accomplished. I knew my tomb, had groped my way all around it, and I knew where a pointed rock jutted out. If I stood on tiptoe I could attach something to it. The silken shawl I wore as a girdle was perfect. It would not tear, dared not tear, for it came from the gods. Aphrodite had given it to her daughter upon her marriage to Cadmus the Theban. In the city this piece of cloth was worshiped as holy. Polyneices had taken it with him when he fled, so as to have something from home about him always. I recovered it from his corpse. It had become black and stiff with blood. No one recognized my girdle as the stolen treasure, and so it was not taken from me. In the cave I kissed it again and again. The last remnant of him. Which would now help me obtain my freedom.

They had left nothing for me to eat, only a jug of wine. I drank it hastily. The wine made me sure of myself and nimble. I rolled a large stone under the jutting rock, knotted the shawl to it, and placed the noose around my neck. Then I kicked away the stone on which I was standing. And the veil held.

I had accepted the idea of being a king's daughter, and it offered me many possibilities. But not until we left Thebes did I wake up, break out of the fetters of my caste, shake off the taboos. On my way through the mountains, alone with the blind man, I found myself, became Antigone. The nights, the hot, dry days, the rustling wind, the dark forests and the gleaming white cliffs, and plants and animals, taught me to think, taught me to feel. At home I had dabbled in the arts, had painted a little, danced a little, played the cithara a little, and composed many poems. I thought myself a poet. Until I was up in the mountains and finally grasped the fact that I was gifted for only one art: being a sister.

I loved many, I loved only one. When Creon gave the order that he was not to be buried, my sorrow turned to hatred. I had no plan and no goal, did not want to unseat Creon or become his successor. I did not want to become anything, simply to be: to accept fate and my fellow human beings. When I set out at night, the children were there. They thronged about me, pushed me forward, shouting and singing. The wind gained strength, became a tempest, yet through its roar I could make out what the children were singing:

> Run, sister, run
> No one holds you back
> The wind blows from the west
> The guards are sound asleep
> Go, sister, go
> Bed him down in peace
> Even if it bring death
> Fulfill the gods' command
> Stay the tyrant's hand
> For our sake make Thebes free

I ran and ran, driven by the fear of discovery. Not until I had sprinkled my brother with earth did my fear vanish. I felt all light inside, perfectly calm. After I had returned to the palace at the first trace of dawn, had taken a bath and was lying exhausted on my bed, I realized that this burial would not suffice. The gods' command had been satisfied, the ritual accomplished. But I had to shout it out for all to hear: He who demands unconditional obedience acts against life.

At noon I ventured forth again. The dead man had been pulled free of the dirt that covered him. I picked up a clod and threw it down next to him. It struck the ground with a dull thud. The guards seized me. They yanked my hair, they beat me until I bled. One of them thrust his foot into me; I keeled over. I felt no pain. The harder they tried to humiliate me, the more I felt my dignity. My joy, my sorrow made me blessed. In this exalted mood I was brought before Creon. He would have liked to cover up the matter, but it was too late. He had no wish to kill me, but he had to do it, lest he lose his credibility with the people. Perhaps he realized that there was no room in Thebes for the two of us. It upset him to see me looking this way. He was fond of me and had probably never seen a woman battered and smeared with blood. We quarreled, and I spoke the sentence that has made me famous for all time, something I find extraordinary, since it merely expresses the obvious. No human being comes into the world to hate. I am not sure whether Creon really heard me. If I wanted love, I would have to go down to Hades, he said, unmoved. Then he burst out: So long as I live, no woman shall rule. But that had not been suggested, I had demanded nothing but equal justice for Polyneices and Eteocles.

I did not approve of Polyneices' attitude. Yet our differences were the source of our fascination for one another. I loved him. Accepted him. Understood him. So alien, so, so close. The questions remained: Why had he not agreed to share the power with Eteocles? Why had he not discussed the matter with him? Why had he chosen war? War is the worst solution. War should never be allowed.

She bends over me. Embraces me. Does not pull away anymore. Stays with me.

You keep searching for my secret, yet it is so simple: Feel and think yourself, not me. Never ask: Do you love me as I love you? Always say: It is I who love you.

Do not resist yourself. Accept. Learn to empty yourself, that you may absorb the fullness of life.

Stay, oh please stay. You can't just abandon me this way. I will fall. You have taken away the net that promised me safety. It was a murder attempt. Why did you not finish the job?

17

My pillow is wet with tears. I am alone. She wants me to accept myself. I strain against that. With all the strength I have left. Thrash around in my bed, pushing away the blanket with my feet. Then I lie quietly. Let my head fall back. Perhaps I am dying. I wait.

It is perfectly still. The door opens softly, and my mother comes into the room. Brushes my forehead with her cool hand. Goes to the table and busies herself there. Brings my medicine. Places her arm behind my back and helps me sit up. Holds out the glass. I drink. Then she lets me sink back into the pillows. For a while I hear her walking back and forth, then she leaves the room. Through the door I hear muffled voices; the family is sitting down to lunch. My parents, my brother, my grandmother. The maid comes from the kitchen to serve them. I lie there motionless. The fever is pleasant. Hovering on the verge of slumber. No enemy can touch me. The family protects me. My fortress.

I am standing with Mother by my sister's grave. At the top her name is carved into the smooth black stone. Below is a large space. ''That's where our names will be inscribed some day,'' Mother says. ''Your sister was seven when she died. As old as you are now. If she hadn't died, you wouldn't be here.'' I owe my life to the death of another human being. My mother weeps. Plucks off a few withered leaves of ivy. Whispers, "She was so lovely. So gentle. My dear, good child." I do not look at the grave. Want to get away from here. I hate the cemetery. Why does no one cry for me?

Mother says, "Just look at your fur slippers—they're all scuffed. You can't run around looking like that."

"But no one sees me."

"One musn't let oneself go, even when one is alone."

She does not let herself go. When she dies, at the age of eighty-six, in her baby-blue nightgown with the two bows at the neck, the person lying there with the death rattle in her throat is a young girl. Blond, naive, winsome. Untouched by the horrors of the world.

When Mother has her lady friends to tea, I am supposed to put on my blue velvet dress, go down to the parlor, and make the rounds, curtsying and shaking hands. Why do I not rebel? Because I think it is not worth the effort. All unsuspecting, I fall into the trap of conforming and receive no answers to the questions that trouble me.

Our dog catches a mouse out in the woods, holds the wriggling creature by the tail and consumes it from one end to the other with obvious relish. I sit on a tree stump and watch. When the dog is finished, he comes to me, stands on his hind legs with his front paws on my knees, and licks my face. I make no attempt to push him away. I love the dog.

Katia and I are playing, cutting out paper dolls and clothes for them. "Give me the light blue one; that one goes with my doll."

"No, stupid, that goes with mine."

"You always want everything for yourself."

"That's not true!"

We hit each other, pull each other's hair, go after each other with the scissors. My nanny breaks up the fight. Immediately we join forces against her.

We are thirteen. Sleep in the same room on a hiking trip. She comes into my bed. Teaches me how to kiss, to make love. Her head is between my thighs, her tongue furiously caressing my delicate membranes. Then I push her off and bury my head in her lap. Our play: passionate, tender, clumsy. Forbidden, delicious games.

We are fourteen. The big subject for us is death. The grand freedom that will preserve us from the awful fate of becoming dull like the grown-ups. We discuss suicide in the same breath as the mountain-climbing expedition scheduled for next Sunday. I sense that Katia is much too greedy for life to take our talk seriously. And then suddenly she is dead, having turned on the gas after a fight with her parents. Katia, the first girl I loved.

I am sixteen. Am lying with René, three years my senior, in his garret room. We are looking at the portfolio of Dutch genre paintings. He shows me a small engraving: a scholar in his study. Everything is in shadow except the bearded old man, who is illuminated by light streaming in the window. "Perhaps it really is a Rembrandt," René says dreamily.

"Where did you get it?"

"I picked it up at the fair for five marks fifty." His long nose twitches with satisfaction. He looks like Echnaton—degenerate, ugly, fascinating.

With René again. He sets up a miniature Sienese altar triptych for me. "It's yours."

"But René, that's much too valuable."

"Too valuable for my girl?" He laughs arrogantly. "Today all I can give you is the altar of an unknown master. But the day is coming when I shall give you something by Duccio or one of the other great names.''

With René again. I am helping him catalogue the most recently acquired items in his collection. There is a knock. Two men enter the room. ''Detective Division,'' says one of them and shows his badge. ''We have a warrant for your arrest.'' René stares at the two. Offers no explanations. Asks no questions.

''What is this all about?'' I ask.

''This gentleman is under arrest because his collection was obtained by theft.'' He is led away between two men. René, the first boy I loved.

A highway, bordered on both sides by trees, lines that converge at the horizon. On the ground deep shadows alternate with long patches of sunlight. I take rapid steps, unencumbered by luggage, and let my arms swing freely. The light spring air is ideal for hiking. I do not know where I am going, have no particular destination, feel strong and vigorous. After a while I see three old people dressed in black walking ahead of me: two men and a woman, leaning heavily on canes. They are already quite close when I notice them. Either I have not been paying attention, or they have just entered the road from a side road. In a moment I will have caught up with them and passed them. But the distance between us remains the same; it even seems to me as if it is growing larger, almost imperceptibly. That is nonsense, must be an illusion. When I stop for a moment, I can tell how slowly they are moving. I quicken my steps, begin to run, or at least I think I am running. I hear my breath, hear myself panting, feel the thumping of my heart, a stabbing in my chest, pain in my knee. For a while I keep it up, then I cannot go on, give up. Sink down on a milestone, slumped over.

After the bombardment of Guernica I write:

We let Guernica's children die
because we are cowards before others' torment.
In silence we await the ruination
with which we shall atone in blood.

Not a very good poem, but a true insight. We know what is coming, wait for it, do nothing, do not flee to safety.

The essay I have to write for the final examination in school: "Lessing's Glorious Role in Reawakening German Consciousness." I have boned up on the writer Gotthold Ephraim Lessing; it is 1929, the year in which we have commemorated the two-hundredth anniversary of his birth. But I have not boned up on nationalistic idiocy. What is "German consciousness"? What is it this preceptor of the human race is supposed to have not only awakened but reawakened, this man whom the Saxons considered a Prussian and the Prussians a Saxon?

On the blackboard our instructions are heavily underlined: The German essay is to be written in German script. That too is German consciousness. So I reluctantly write in German script that Lessing, who regarded patriotism as a heroic foible, was transformed by others into a national hero, for which he should be neither blamed nor praised. I present this thesis in a four-page essay, writing that Lessing's overriding concern was tolerance, something that at no time could be subsumed under German consciousness. I close with Hofmannsthal's words: "His significance for the nation lies in his critical attitude toward the very concept."

I receive a 5 for the essay, the lowest grade. "Complete misinterpretation of the topic."

I misinterpret the topic, the topic of Lessing, the

topic of Antigone. I want to write about her, want to be her, but when the opportunity presents itself to take arms against hate, I leave the dead unburied.

I am standing in the dressing room in front of a large mirror, wearing a gray dress I like very much. I slowly pivot to show it off. Mother, who is sitting on a stool observing me attentively through her lorgnon, says, "The red one suits you better."

"But the gray one is more chic."

"You and your idea of chic. It's too somber. You can wear things like that when you are old. We'll take the red one."

Trudy on the telephone: "My poor sister in Cologne hasn't much longer to live. I told you about her cancer of the pancreas. I don't plan to go to see her—I can't take the strain. But I suppose I will have to go to the funeral. She wants to be buried in our parents' plot. The proprieties mean so much to her. She had our father's second wife and the woman's homosexual son from her first marriage—and the son's boyfriend—moved to a different grave because she says she doesn't want to share a grave with such people. Well, you can't exactly blame her."

O tomb, O wedding chamber. I do not know, do not want to know, whether there were ovens in Mauthausen. Whether they piled up the bodies in a mass grave. Whether they ripped his heart out of his chest and threw it to the dogs. It does not matter to me. A heart—a muscle that pumps blood through the body so long as a person is alive.

I am in Paris, staying with Waiki's brother and his wife. I borrow their car to visit a friend, and return without mishap. But in the evening when all of us plan to drive somewhere, I cannot recall where I parked the car. Desperate, unsuccessful forays into nearby streets and underground garages. My mind is blank, becomes more and more blank. Dying must be like this, the process of dissolution has begun, the world is slipping away from me, the beloved world which I cannot hold on to.

I try to think the unthinkable, to experience the physicists' speculations about the world as finite. Everything will come to a halt. That thought produces a deep sense of satisfaction.

I am lying on a mattress in the dining room of a ship. We are in a heavy storm, and I am clutching a bucket, into which I vomit. Whenever I find that I can only gag, I stick my index and middle fingers into my throat. My stomach is empty, but slimy bile still comes up. Then the dizziness and nausea can be borne for a little while. Waiki towers over me, green in the face. He wants to take away my pail. "Just for a moment."

"Go to hell."

He shrugs, walks away. At that moment there is the thunder of artillery, grenades strike us, I am jammed in among other people; those next to me are hit and sink to the ground, arms and legs go flying through the air. I am standing on the swaying ship, see Waiki running toward me. Another hit, and he is no longer there. I stand where I was, with blood pouring down me, over my face, my hands.

Ah, human beings, you murderers.

In my garden in the Ticino I am planting a little camellia. It has flat pink blossoms, the petals arranged in circles around the center. For a while I gaze at it with intense pleasure. Then I reach for my spade. With my first strenuous thrust into the sod I am filled with keen certainty that I am digging my own grave, with the execution squad at my back. The soldiers have rested their rifle butts on the ground, are supporting their weight on their guns. Mechanically I lift the last clods of loose, dark earth out of the hole, pour in water, lower the plant into it, fill the hole with the soil I dug out, and tamp it down with my feet. The soldiers are gone, the camellia stands there, swaying slightly in the breeze.

I am on my knees, weeding my rock garden, tossing the weeds into a willow basket next to me. Then it is no longer my sun-drenched slope; I am kneeling on a flat expanse of earth in a gray land. There is a stench of burnt flesh. I hack and pluck for my very life, which I have saved by lying, saying that I was a trained gardener. If the commandant's wife is not satisfied with my work, I shall be led off to the gas chamber.

I heave lengths of firewood onto my shoulder and carry them up from the lower forest to the cellar. Always two at a time. They are not particularly heavy, but I walk cautiously and keep my eyes on the ground, so as not to stumble on the steps. I mount the steep Death Steps, a block of stone on my shoulder. It is crushing me, I cannot go on.

Trudy on the telephone: "The dollar is falling, my boyfriend has flown to America to buy up real estate. Now is the time to grab it, he says, because soon it will be worth much more. He promised to bring me back a mink coat. Isn't that terrific?"

The manager takes me on a tour of Waiki's factory. Before the war, when I worked here, everything was done by hand. Now the bottles are filled, sealed, and packaged by machine, the whole process fast and hygienic. The few women who work here take the packaged drugs and stack them on large tables. For five days a week, eight hours a day, they reach to the right and lower to the left. Reach right for me and lower left for me. For my house in the Ticino, my car, my trips. I flee, screaming.

I am standing in a meadow, playing with children. They throw me a ball. I hold out my hands, but no matter how hard I try I cannot catch it. Either it bounces off my fingers or I close my hands on nothingness. The children laugh at me.

I am writing with great concentration for hours on end, without eating, without drinking. The ashtray gets fuller and fuller. All my problems are solved, and Antigone has taken on the radiance I always wanted for myself.

At night I get up and burn the pages I wrote during the day.

Trudy on the telephone: "I'd like to leave the Church; just think of all the money I pour down its throat. But how can you leave something you've belonged to all your life, and your parents and grandparents as well? And how can you be buried without a pastor? No, unfortunately it just can't be done."

Wearing my black velveteen slacks and my black-and-white embroidered Indian jacket, with Mother's baroque pearls around my neck, I go to hear *Fidelio*.

I get through the first act all right, although I find it hard to bear prisons where people are tortured, even on the stage. During the intermission I roam through the foyer, watching the people in their finery, unable to feel any link with them. What are they doing here? What am I doing here myself? Then Florestan sings, sings his aria very beautifully, with piercing sweetness: "An angel like Leonora, my dear beloved wife, will lead me to freedom in the land without strife." But instead of the overweight tenor, made up to look haggard, standing in his operatic prison, I see words in shaky letters: *Forever yours, Waiki*. The last words in his last letter. Out of which the censor had snipped two lines. I shall never know what they were supposed to tell me. After the aria Florestan falls to the ground, and stays there motionless while the audience claps, stomps, and shouts. I stand up, pressing a handkerchief to my mouth, and flee.

Antigone kneels before Haverkamp, pleading with him to help her.

"I would do it gladly, Princess, but I cannot. Creon embodies the State, and without the State, life as a community is not possible."

"What harm can it do the community if a dead man is buried?"

"It is a matter of principle. Obeying a law is a symbol of submission. Just as for you, dear child, your deed was a symbol of rebellion."

"Not of rebellion. Of humane behavior."

"It comes to the same thing. Humane behavior is always rebellion."

Trudy on the telephone: "When they catch a terrorist, they should put him up against the nearest wall. If an innocent bystander gets caught in the cross fire now and then, that's just too bad."

Waiki strokes the dog, kisses it. "Stop that," I say, "he belongs to Urs and me." Waiki turns and walks away, and the dog runs after him.

I am scrambling up a sheer mountain face, groping with my hands and feet, dragging myself up, feeling the cliff, feeling myself. The piece of rock I am hanging on to gives way, and I try to press it back into the stone, lest it break away just when I need it most. I am terrified, mortally terrified. Full of elation.

Before Hitler: My parents are away on a trip. Three of us are standing in the living room around the table lamp with its dark red velvet shade: Klaus, stubbly hair above his young, intelligent face, lanky Doris, with her wry Berlin humor, and I. Klaus takes a syringe and three ampules out of his briefcase. Says to me, "We brought one for you too. It will be like no trip you have ever taken, you will have incredible dreams.'' I am trembling with curiosity, dying to experience those dreams, yet I know that if I try this, I will have to give up mountain-climbing and skiing. Why sacrifice my special perilous paradise for something new but untried? If I say no, I will only be confirming the others' notion that my bourgeois origins prevent me from ever being one of them; I have always suffered from this inability to jump over my own shadow, can see the scorn in their eyes. What is cowardice here? What is courage? Without a word I turn and leave the room.

During Hitler: Both of them emigrate immediately, although they are not Jewish. Klaus, a writer and journalist, indefatigable opponent of the Third Reich, first in Europe, then in the United States, finally becomes an American soldier. Doris, first in the Spanish Civil War, on the side of the Republicans, then in the French Resistance, spends the last years of the war in the Maquis.

After Hitler: Klaus goes to Cannes to meet Doris and there commits suicide. Doris drinks herself to death. Their last letters, begging for a little money, arrive from shelters for the homeless. Both of them died of our times. Truer to themselves than I.

I play with my pills as if they were pearls. My palms are dusted with white powder. I lick it off. The bitter taste is pleasant. Calming.

We are holding a farewell party at our teacher's a few days before we graduate from secondary school. We play music, recite poems, and talk, eager for what the future will bring. As we are on our way home, detachments of the SA march past us. As yet without uniforms, in windbreakers, shorts, and white kneesocks. Swastika bands on their arms. They are singing ''When Jewish blood spurts from the knife.'' My girl friends look the other way in embarrassment and say not a word. I am frightened, not only of the braying men but also of the silent girls.

The train is racing through the black night. The whistle wails. Waiki and I are shaken awake, thrown against each other, torn apart. We cling tightly to each other, do not know our destination.

My feet swollen—from undernourishment—I walk the twelve kilometers to where Mother is in hiding. There I take off my shoes and cannot get them on again. Am lent a pair of wooden clogs. I walk back in them. They hurt from the very beginning, and with every step the pain grows, until finally I am leaving a trail of blood behind me like a wounded deer. I dare not stop to rest; the curfew is at seven o'clock, and I must be home by then. I walk and walk, counting the steps: one hundred, then I stop; eighty, then I stop; fifty, then I stop. I bite my lips to keep from screaming. Blood drips from my lip as well. Antigone walks beside me, saying, ''Come along now, come.'' She is a balm, a mild breeze, freshly fallen snow in the mountains, a tower of courage that supports me. The war cannot continue much more than a few weeks, perhaps only days; the Germans are done for. The moment I have long dreaded is near, the moment when the others will return. But there are too many who will never return. Waiki is only one in an endless procession. No joy is felt, only sorrow. A slick of oil on the sea, spoiling everything with its putrid ooze.

Long tables are set up on the platform in the freight station. Tables with typewriters and stacks of paper. Behind these tables sit the members of the Jewish Council. In front of the tables stand the countless Jews just rounded up in a huge raid. Gray, with the terrified faces of people deprived of sleep. I am typing out names, dates of birth, addresses. I label the house keys and place them in a little basket. Barely have time to look up. The SS captain who calls out the prisoners' names is positioned behind me. The process cannot go fast enough to satisfy him.

"Next. Name?"

"Antigone."

"Antigone who?"

"Just Antigone." I look at her. She smiles. Looks lovelier than I have ever seen her. I am alarmed by her air of determination.

"Address?"

"Thebes."

"Thebes Street. What number?"

"Thebes is a city, not a street."

"A city in Holland?"

"No, in Greece. Didn't you learn that in school?"

"Now, don't get smart with me!" I can sense how nervous this girl makes him. He cannot place her. He slowly walks around the long table and stops. In a moment he will strike her. But he does not touch her, cannot break through the magic circle around her. Very solemnly she says, "I cannot share in love, but in hatred." Then she pulls a revolver out of her dress, aims it at the SS captain, who stands there rigid, and presses the trigger. The shot makes a sharp, dry sound. Silence. No corpse lies there. There is no blood. From all sides appear men in long Goebbels-style coats, with caps whose visors shade their faces. They approach Antigone.

A large square, with bumpy cobblestones, a few stunted, bare trees, gray and wretched. In the background the prison, sooty red brick, tiny barred windows. Not a concentration camp. No electrified barbed wire, no watchtowers, only high walls. No mountain tomb.

I am freezing, wearing a coat that is not nearly

heavy enough, do not know whom or what I am waiting for, or why I am standing here. I swing my arms, but that does not warm me. My fingers are chapped and swollen, I grope in my pockets for gloves, find none. See no one, but have the feeling I am being watched from the barred windows.

The heavy gate of the prison opens a crack, and a little figure slips out, in a yellow dress, her feet in sandals. She quickly runs toward me, throws herself into my arms, weeping. My face is wet with her tears. The moisture freezes on my cheeks. I press Antigone to me, try to cover her with my coat. Why not take her away to a warm place, to the shelter of a house? I have orders to stay here. I desperately try to recall who gave the order.

My memory is obliterated. Where do I come from? Where do I belong? In what country? In what place?

Suddenly I let her go, and she falls to the ground, remains lying where she fell. I take to my heels, running, running.

18

I get up, splash cold water on my face in the bathroom, slip into my bathrobe, and go into the living room. I gaze out the window into the evening darkness. Down below, cars pass, an unending chain of lights. On the opposite side of the street, at the corner of the park where the whores strut back and forth waiting for customers, I can glimpse the vacant lot with the bulldozed ruins, where the rats live. To its left a Quonset hut, which houses a bar. A drunk comes out, staggers around, stumbles into the hole dug by the bulldozer, falls down, sits up, then lies down on the ground, pulls his coat around him, and does not move again. Behind him the blank white wall of a newly constructed building. The roof of the bar intersects the white surface. To the right is the neoclassical portal of the bombed city library, left standing as a monument, a reminder. Between it and the white wall glistens a narrow strip of the Main River. A dimly lit barge is being towed slowly upriver, its red running light on my side. Farther off on Sachsenhaus Mountain is the illuminated tower of the brewery, a giant silo. It is all atrociously ugly.

I feel the ugliness, am one with the ugliness, which swirls around me. I let it wrap itself around me, accept it, accept myself, am happy.

And tomorrow?

AUTHOR'S NOTE

The unpublished eyewitness account of the liquidation of the Piotrkow ghetto was placed at my disposal by the heirs of its author, Friedrich Hellmund. It appears here in slightly abridged form.

Friedrich Hellmund, a writer and theater director, was born in 1903 in Latvia and disappeared in 1945 in Poland. From 1911 to 1920 he attended the Odenwald School, then studied history and German literature, receiving his doctorate at the age of twenty-one at the University of Frankfurt. He served as a noncommissioned officer during the war with the 954th Protection Batallion.

TRANSLATOR'S NOTE

Page 16: The first quotation from Sophocles' *Antigone* is taken from the translation by Elizabeth Wyckoff in the volume *Sophocles I* (Chicago: University of Chicago Press, 1954).

Page 77: The quotation from Bertolt Brecht's *Threepenny Opera* is taken from the translation done by Marc Blitzstein for the first American performance of the Brecht–Weill play.

Page 113: The quotation from Eugen Kogon's *The Theory and Practice of Hell* is taken from the translation done by Neinz Norden (New York: Farrar, Straus & Giroux, 1950).

NEW FROM  AVON BARD

DISTINGUISHED MODERN FICTION

SENT FOR YOU YESTERDAY
John Edgar Wideman   82644-5 $3.50
In SENT FOR YOU YESTERDAY, John Edgar Wideman, "one of America's premier writers of fiction" (*The New York Times*), tells the passion of ordinary lives, the contradictions, perils, pain and love which are the blood and bone of everybody's America. "Perhaps the most gifted black novelist in his generation." *The Nation*

Also from Avon Bard: **DAMBALLAH** (78519-6 $2.95) and **HIDING PLACE** (78501-3 $2.95)

THE LEOPARD'S TOOTH
William Kotzwinkle   62869-4 $2.95
A supernatural tale of a turn-of-the-century archaeological expedition to Africa and the members' breathtaking adventures with the forces of good and evil, by "one of today's most inventive writers." (Playboy).

DREAM CHILDREN
Gail Godwin   62406-0 $3.50
Gail Godwin, the bestselling author of A MOTHER AND TWO DAUGHTERS (61598-3/$3.95), presents piercing, moving, beautifully wrought fiction about women possessed of imagination, fantasy, vision and obsession who live within the labyrinths of their minds. "Godwin is a writer of enormous intelligence, wit and compassion...DREAM CHILDREN is a fine place to start catching up with an extraordinary writer." *Saturday Review*

Available wherever paperbacks are sold or directly from the publisher. Include $1.00 per copy for postage and handling: allow 6-8 weeks for delivery. Avon Books. Dept BP. Box 767 Rte 2. Dresden. TN 38225.

NEW FROM ▮▮ AVON BARD

DISTINGUISHED MODERN FICTION

THE VILLA GOLITSYN
Piers Paul Read   61929-6/$3.50
In this taut suspense novel by bestselling and award-winning author Piers Paul Read, an Englishman asked to spy on an old friend uncovers a shocking truth leading to death at a luxurious, secluded villa in southern France. "Substantial and vivid…The sexual intrigue reaches a high pitch." *The New York Times*

BENEFITS: A NOVEL
Zöe Fairbairns   63164-4/$2.95
Published in Great Britain to critical acclaim, this chilling futuristic novel details the rise to power in a future England of the "Family" party, which claims to cure the economic and social problems by controlling reproduction and institutionalizing motherhood. "A successful and upsetting novel." *The London Sunday Times* "Chilling Orwellian vision of society…an intelligent and energetic book." *The London Observer*

TREASURES ON EARTH
Carter Wilson   63305-1/$3.95
In 1911, a young photographer joins a Yale expedition to the Andes in search of a lost Incan city. In the midst of a spectacular scientific find—Machu Picchu—he makes a more personal discovery and finds the joy of forbidden love which frees his heart and changes his life. "Its power is so great, we may be witnessing the birth of a classic." *Boston Globe* "A fine new novel…beautifully and delicately presented." *Publishers Weekly*

Available wherever paperbacks are sold or directly from the publisher. Include 50¢ per copy for postage and handling; allow 6-8 weeks for delivery. Avon Books, Mail Order Dept., 224 West 57th St., N.Y., N.Y. 10019

III Bard 3-83

NEW FROM AVON 🎭 BARD
DISTINGUISHED
MODERN FICTION

DR. RAT   63990-4/$3.95
William Kotzwinkle
This chilling fable by the bestselling author of THE FAN MAN and FATA MORGANA is an unforgettable indictment of man's inhumanity to man, and to all living things. With macabre humor and bitter irony, Kotzwinkle uses Dr. Rat as mankind's apologist in an animal experimentation laboratory grotesquely similar to a Nazi concentration camp.

ON THE WAY HOME   63131-8/$3.50
Robert Bausch
This is the powerful, deeply personal story of a man who came home from Vietnam and what happened to his family.
"A strong, spare, sad and beautiful novel, exactly what Hemingway should write, I think, if he'd lived through the kind of war we make now."   John Gardner
"A brilliant psychological study of an intelligent, close family in which something has gone terribly and irretrievably wrong."   *San Francisco Chronicle*

AGAINST THE STREAM   63693-X/$4.95
James Hanley
"James Hanley is a most remarkable writer....Beneath this book's calm flow there is such devastating emotion."
The New York Times Book Review
This is the haunting, illuminating novel of a young child whose arrival at the isolated stone mansion of his mother's family unleashes their hidden emotions and forces him to make a devastating choice.

Buy these books at your local bookstore or use this coupon for ordering:

Avon Books. Dept BP. Box 767. Rte 2. Dresden. TN 38225
Please send me the book(s) I have checked above. I am enclosing $ . . . .
(please add $1.00 to cover postage and handling for each book ordered to a maximum of three dollars). *Send check or money order—no cash or C.O.D.'s please.* Prices and numbers are subject to change without notice. Please allow six to eight weeks for delivery.

Name ....

Address ....

City .... **State/Zip** ....

Bard 9-83